The
Perrely Plight

YOUNG AMERICA BOOK CLUB
Presents

PETER JOHN STEPHENS

The Perrely Plight

———

A Mystery at Sturbridge

Drawings by R. D. Rice

ATHENEUM   1965   NEW YORK

To Pixie and Pixiekyn

Contents

Gib Meets Philander Perrely

GIB had always been curious about the Perrelys, especially about Philander Perrely. And at last it looked as if his chance to find out something had come.

It was a summer morning in 1836 and time to bring in the hay. Gib's father owned quite a bit of land a few miles from the village of Sturbridge, Massachusetts, in the low-lying area across the Quinebaug River. This was very close to where Philander Perrely lived. There were a few farm houses there, sunk at the bottom of the valley that people called the Hollow. The Hollow had a bad reputation. No child from the village of Sturbridge was ever allowed to go there alone.

3

But Gib was now twelve years old and tall for his age, though slight. Perhaps his father had decided twelve meant something special. Certainly something had happened. For yesterday he had said, "You'll have Marybell in your charge tomorrow, Gibeon." He was to ride the mare down to the hayfield at noon with food for the men, and he would be passing the Hollow for the first time alone.

Before dawn his father had left for the fields. Quite a gathering of men and their carts had set off with him, all the men very willing to help Doctor Martindale bring in his hay.

Gib's mother and Cousin Lovina were busy preparing part of the men's dinner, with the help of some neighbors. Gib would carry the food in saddlebags down to the field at noon.

Gib was out in the barn getting the mare ready. She was a frisky old thing, and liked nothing better than a brisk gallop. This day though, Gib would have to hold her in a bit, since he would be carrying the haymakers' dinner.

"Balance the saddlebags, Gibeon," his father had warned him. "You can give extra weight to the light side with a few stones if you need."

Soon they were packed and on their way. Marybell seemed unusually well-behaved. She moved steadily along the rough dirt road, which led them past the miser Petit's farm and down towards the covered bridge.

They would soon be across the river and on the lower

road. There Gib planned to hold the mare to a very slow pace so that he could stare at Philander's house to his heart's content. Perhaps he would catch a glimpse of Philander himself.

The folk in the village did not talk much about the Perrelys, for the Perrelys were among the "shiftless, low-livin' folk" of the Hollow. That is what people said of them. "Shiftless" meant they didn't farm properly or didn't farm at all. "Low-livin' " meant they didn't look after their homes or keep themselves neat and clean, didn't send their children to school, or, what was worse, didn't go to church on the Sabbath.

This was all Gib and his closest friend Timothy knew. And no questions they asked seemed to bring answers that told them any more. But to Gib and Timothy it seemed that there must be something more. Why should their parents be so determined to keep them from the Hollow?

Certainly everything down in the Hollow looked very untidy to Gib. Most of the homes were little more than old-fashioned, unpainted wood shacks, and the land was so overgrown it almost seemed as if the Hollow would soon be swallowed up by a returning tide of wilderness and Indians. But all of this did not seem reason enough for such strong feeling—a feeling that seemed to be directed especially against the Perrelys. Then, too, there was something strangely different about the Perrely house; Gib intended to scan it closely as he went by alone.

Twice Gib had actually seen Philander. Once was on one of those rare occasions when he came into the village. He had appeared at the blacksmith's shop while Gib was standing watching Mr. Tibbals and his sons working at the double forge. Philander was six or seven years older than Gib. He was tall, as tall as the giant blacksmith and his two giant sons, though not as broad in the shoulders. He had appeared at the door like a shadow, very solemn, and had spoken in a low unhurried voice.

He wanted a piece of iron shaped in a peculiar way. No one knew what for, not even Mr. Tibbals. Philander waited as he watched over the work being done for him. Then he wrapped the piece of iron in a cloth and walked away with the long slow stride of a hunter.

The other time Gib had been riding in the chaise on his one journey to Boston. Philander had been standing motionless on the lower road. He had been hunting and was obviously annoyed at the intrusion of a horse and carriage. Gib's father had frowned, but to Gib's disappointment he had said nothing.

Philander fascinated all the boys. The fact that Philander was an expert with his rifle had a great deal to do with this. He was known to scorn the use of a fowling piece when he hunted birds. He preferred his rifle, and that, as everyone knew, meant the use of a bullet, not shot. It meant a sharp, quick, and accurate aim.

Some said it was the result of an invention, something he had thought up that made the gun ten times more accurate. In fact the village folk had heard the peddler say so. That was Pardon Perrely, Philander's father. But Pardon Perrely said many things, and no one could tell whether he was joking or not. Philander said nothing and was seldom seen, so no one knew if there was truth in the story or not.

Gib had wondered and talked a lot about it with his friend Timothy; but neither of them dared search out Philander and ask him. For if their fathers found out, they would be punished for going into the valley.

Now, when the chance had come at last for learning something, Timothy was away visiting an aunt in Boston. Gib would have to have his adventure alone.

Approaching the bridge, Gib eased Marybell to a walk. The river was not wide or deep here. It was a rapid, foaming stretch, plunging and dodging among haphazard rocks. It was better for Marybell that she could not see what was going on below. The covering over the bridge hid everything from view.

It was like passing through a barn with doors open at both ends. The wood was fresh, unpainted. The bridge was only a few years old.

As he moved slowly through, Gib looked at the truss that held the bridge up and wondered at how simple it was. The truss looked to him like the lattice work of a garden fence. The pieces as they crossed were pinned together with heavy wooden pegs.

He was so busy admiring the bridge that he did not

notice Willis Pickle until he was almost there.

"What ye dreamin' at?" asked Willis with a laugh that echoed through the bridge.

Gib did not like Willis. He was a little older, and he was fat and self-satisfied. His perpetual self-assurance made Gib feel that he was being laughed at.

"Nothing." Gib tried to sound superior.

"I'll race ye, Gib."

Gib looked at Willis, shocked. Was he trying to make a joke? They were both on their way to feed the haymakers and it was almost time to be there.

"Are ye afraid to," Willis jeered, "with that old haybag of yours?"

What a way to talk about Marybell! She twitched her ears, and Gib instinctively put a soothing hand on her neck.

Willis laughed again. He was sitting astride a rather large and powerful-looking beast. He glanced down with obvious pride. "My uncle's, he is. Better'n a racer. Ye'd not have a chance."

Gib was aroused. Marybell was in the mood for a gallop. Why not try her? He would certainly like to knock Willis down a bit.

Willis wasn't satisfied with a straight race. He insisted on their going back up the hill. "To give 'em a start," he said. They would race down the hill, manipulate the bridge crossing, and end the course where the road passed the house of Pardon Perrely the peddler. It would be unwise to go beyond that, for their fathers would see what they were doing from the hay-fields.

Gib clenched his teeth and grimly nodded himself into all Willis proposed. They went back up the hill in silence, Gib trying to keep his heart from beating too loud.

They ranged their horses round. "One, two . . ." Without waiting for the "three" they both spurred their horses to a wild and plunging gallop down the slope, raising the dust in dense clouds behind them. Gib leaned forward, the wind roaring about his ears, vaguely saying to himself that this was dangerous. Should Marybell stumble . . .

But she didn't. Gib had nothing to do but to hold on, while Marybell flew downward, taking the lead from Willis' horse almost at once.

Gib could hear Willis shouting wildly for more speed, but Marybell was gleefully kicking her dust in his face.

The dark mouth of the covered bridge rushed to meet them, and Gib, in an instinctive gesture, ducked his head down to go through. At that moment something went wrong.

Marybell took fright, veered sharply to one side, and Gib felt the saddlebags slipping. He clutched wildly to prevent them from falling, and the next moment found himself rolling down the riverbank, stopping just at the river's edge. The breath was knocked out of him. He couldn't get up at once.

He heard a wild cry of triumph from Willis and the thundering of hoofs as his great beast roared across the bridge and tore on round the bend in the road.

Slowly Gib pulled himself together. His knee was bruised; and one shoulder seemed out of joint. Where was Marybell and the dinner for the workers in the field?

Gib listened. There was no sound now above the ever-rushing waters. Willis had left him to his fate. Marybell had vanished. What would his father say? Almost sobbing with pain and desperation, Gib hauled himself up the bank and stood in the center of the road, utterly forlorn. In the silence, the leaves of an aspen waved like a crowd of onlookers.

It was then that he saw Marybell, coming toward him along the path out of the woods. But she was not coming of her own accord. She was being led by a tall, quiet, serious youth. Gib's heart leaped. It was Philander Perrely. Gib ran toward them, forgetting the soreness of his knee and shoulder. "You caught Marybell!" he cried out. "Thank you."

Philander looked quite grave as he handed the bridle over, and Gib thought he was going to lecture him on being careless. But all he said was, "Hain't no call to thank me. Jest happened to see the race, that's all."

Gib's face fell. "You saw me fall off then?"

Philander didn't answer that. He gave Marybell a pat, "Right spunky little racer, Gib."

"You know who I am?" asked Gib.

"Of course. Doctor Martindale's boy."

"Did you see how she was winning?"

Philander nodded briefly and turned to go.

Gib hurriedly thought of something else to say. "You're Philander Perrely, aren't you? Do they call you Phil for short?"

Philander turned to face Gib and gave him a piercing gaze. "My name's Philander."

Before Gib could recover, Philander had disappeared into the woods, swinging his gun with his left hand.

His gun! Gib realized he had forgotten to look at the gun.

Gib tended to Marybell and was relieved to find that the saddlebags were in order. He would have to hurry now to get to the fields. As he went through the covered bridge and out along the lower road at a smart pace, Gib wondered desperately whether he had offended Philander.

He tried not to slow down as he passed the Perrely house. But even so he could see that the building was not at all like the other homes in the Hollow, for it was quite a large house. It even had an imposing iron gate and a drive. But if it had been elegant once, it was far from that now. Even a quick glance, which was all Gib could give it, showed that it was sadly in need of repair. Its color had faded from red to a dirty pink in those places where the paint had not peeled off altogether. Some of the windows on the upper floor were broken. Trees and bushes had grown up around the house and over the roof as if they were trying to swallow it up. The impression was gloomy and foreboding, like a haunted house ought to look.

There was no sign of life there that Gib could see. He knew that Pardon Perrely was away selling his goods, perhaps as far south as Virginia or the Carolinas or north into Canada. There was no knowing where a peddler would go. But Philander's mother was there, Gib knew; and he had a sister too. Gib had never seen either of them.

When Gib arrived at his father's field, he found the men just in the act of breaking off their work. Several carts were piled high with loads already, the oxen hitched to the back of the carts to keep them from getting too restless. Everyone was in very good spirits. No one noticed that Gib's part of the dinner had almost not arrived.

Willis had a grin on his face from ear to ear. "Told ye I'd win," he said.

Gib concealed his resentment and said off-handedly, "I saw Philander Perrely."

Willis looked at him sharply, and Gib knew he had him envious for a moment.

"Did he show you his gun?"

"He had it with him," said Gib in triumph, as he turned and walked away.

There was little time after that to think of the Perrelys, for Gib had to help with the hay. It had been cut and raked into small heaps at intervals across the field, and men were pitching it from the heaps up on the wagons. Other men stood up on the loads, stowing and stamping to get the hay packed well down. When a pile was loaded, some one would cry "geddup," and the oxen would move on without coaxing to the next pile.

Gib wished he could do the loading, standing high up on the hay like that; but he was set to rake after, drawing the whisps and shreds of hay left by the pitchers-on. He had to use a huge wooden rake, which he held so that the teeth would not catch in the ground but lie almost flat with it. He had to work fast to draw his hay to the next heap before it was all pitched.

It was not an easy job, and there were no resting; for the oxen and their carts moved relentlessly on. Willis was doing the raking in the next line; and a kind of race began, as it always did with Willis. Each raking was an effort to see who would get to the pile ahead with the most first.

The next day, Gib got up very early. He was roused by the sound of his father driving off in the chaise and decided to get up and do some of his log chopping. When he got downstairs, he found Lovina sighing and growling in the kitchen. She had buried the embers of the fire the evening before in the ashes to keep them burning overnight, but they had gone out. Gib's grandmother, who slept in the bedroom off the kitchen, was stirring, and her bones needed warming most of the time. She would not be pleased to find no fire in the large open fireplace.

"I'll set a new fire going," Gib told her. It would delay him on his log chopping, but he liked the mystery of making a spark by striking steel against flint and aiming the spark at the precious little pile of tinder. It took some skill to make it catch, even with expert blowing on it. He did it well, and soon got the fire burning merrily.

Before the approach of winter, the shed back of the house had to be stocked high with firewood from the logs his father had brought down from the hills. Gib had set himself so many logs to saw and chop a day. It was his job. His father did not mind how he did it as long as the work got done. But this day he wanted to get the quota done early, for he had a plan.

After he had been at it for about two hours, his mother called him in for breakfast. By that time, he was really hungry.

When he came into the house, he found that his mother, Granny Hope, and Lovina had already eaten. His father had gone off to tend a patient and would not be back for a long time.

"You seemed to be working so hard out there, I didn't call you in before now. You are a good worker, Gib, just like your father."

Gib felt a little flustered, as he always did at praise, and didn't say anything. He just smiled.

"Lovina put your breakfast in the sitting room, Gib,

so you'd be out of her way."

Gib moved out of the kitchen, glad indeed to be out
of Lovina's way, as well as out of the way of Granny
Hope, sitting on the high-backed settle almost in the
fire. Granny Hope disapproved of boys!

As he sat at the table to eat, his mother settled herself by the window. She had been spinning wool, but she
did not pick up the wool now. Instead she sat looking
across at her son, smiling at him and studying him. The
light from the window lit up her hair like a halo. Gib
thought his mother very pretty.

The Martindales were one of the important families
of Sturbridge. Gib's father was a deacon, as well as one
of the three selectmen who governed the village. For
these reasons, Lydia Martindale had to dress well, and
she did. She loved to sit for hours before a spinning
wheel or at her needlework, but she did not like to cook
or tend to the chores about the house. This she left to
enormous, crotchety Lovina. Lovina was a distant
cousin of hers who had come to live with the Martindales long before Gib was born, and who ruled the roost
in the kitchen.

"What are you going to do today, Gib?" his mother
asked. "After you get finished with your wood-chopping?"

"Perhaps I'll try to find herbs for Lovina. She's been
coaxing me to."

"That will be nice," said his mother, with an abstract
air, which made Gib see that she was going off with

her thoughts.

"Why is the Perrely house different from the others in the Hollow?" Gib asked daringly.

His mother looked startled. "Oh, Gib, I wouldn't go near there!"

"Is there something wrong with it?"

"But such low-living people!" she said vaguely.

Gib wanted to argue, but something made him stop.

"You will have to ask your father," she said suddenly and picked up the wool in both hands, with her foot on the treadle preparing to spin.

Gib thought about it all morning, after he went back to his wood-chopping. It seemed very mysterious, and of course made him more curious than ever.

A House with a Mystery

LOVINA exclaimed at the thought of the herbs. The Martindales had their own herb garden, like most of the well-ordered families in Sturbridge. But Lovina was never content unless she could add some wild herbs to her list.

"I'll get you dinner afore ye go," she said happily.

"What do you know about the Perrelys, Lovina," tried Gib, as he gulped down his food. Luckily, Granny Hope was resting in her room, or she would have gone off into a stream of violent words against the Perrelys.

As it was, Lovina cried out violently enough, "Perrelys, Perrelys! Why ye allus wantin' to know 'bout

18

them Perrelys fur? Shifty, no good lot. Hmpf!"

Gib thought of it, laughing out loud, as he trekked down toward the river, a basket on either arm. Lovina wanted pennyroyal to dry out in the garret. It was good for cramps and for colds, she said. Gib knew where to find it. The search would take him near the Perrely house, but there was nothing wrong with going there, he reasoned, when it was for Lovina's sake. The meadows down there were the best place. There was no disturbing of the ground by plowing, for the Perrelys didn't care to plow. Pardon Perrely peddled goods up and down the country, while Philander hunted, trapped, or fished in the Quinebaug to keep the family alive. Since it was rare to see deer or bear, Gib guessed that Philander could not do much better than woodchuck and rabbit, an occasional raccoon, and perhaps beaver for their meals.

Gib's mind was so occupied as he strolled through the tall meadowland grass, that he was quite startled when a girl about his own age jumped up from where she had been sitting. Like a flushed pheasant, she scampered off, dark loose hair flying, her long skirt held in her hands. She crossed a small stretch of meadow and disappeared behind a clump of brush.

Gib smiled and resumed his walking. But the moment he approached the bushes, he found himself confronted by a tall woman dressed in plain black. Layers of colored beads hung about her neck, in the fashion of an Indian woman. She stood in his way, glaring sternly at him out of her black eyes.

"Good day to you, ma'am," Gib said quickly, not knowing what else he should say.

She continued to look at him in silence, very gravely. Gib thought of the little band of Indians who came in canoes each spring, down to where the river was wide, and sat about in torn blankets and high black hats. Gib had always felt sorry for these Indians. They seemed to have lost all purpose, and everyone avoided them.

The girl he had seen before came shyly into view and sidled up to the woman, then stood staring at him.

The woman now spoke in a low throaty voice, without friendliness, "What ye come lookin' fur, boy?"

Gib answered hastily, "Lovina wants herbs to dry in the garret. I told her I'd see if I could find some of what she wants down in these bottom lands."

"Herbs fur what?"

"For medicines, ma'am," Gib said as polite as he could.

"These medicines are mine. This land here belongs to us'n."

She said this so quietly that Gib was not sure at first of her meaning. She continued to look at him, almost as if her eyes could go through him. Her words had been as flat as the statement of a fact. It meant, he suddenly realized, that this was the Indian wife of Pardon Perrely, a woman few had spoken to and no one wanted to speak to.

"There ain't no call fur village folks to say nothin'

to me, and I ain't got a word to give to them. We kin get along well enough, long as we don't mix in each other's business. I'm sure your pa understands that, and I'm certain I do. There's an end then."

"But ma'am . . . ," he started to speak, but stopped, for he could see it was useless. He turned around and started back the way he had come.

He came to a farm gate. It was half rotten with age and disuse, with tall weeds growing all about it. As he climbed the rail, he suddenly noticed someone watching him. On the other side of the gate, solemn and silent, stood the girl he had seen before. He paused, resting high on the gate.

The girl did not move so he lifted one leg over and sat on the gate, waiting to see what she would do. It seemed to him that she was about to turn again and run off like a frightened fawn.

He smiled at her, which seemed to encourage her, for she moved a little closer and said in a shy voice, "I'm sorry my ma spoke to you so. She don't like folks around, I guess."

Gib replied seriously, "It's no matter." Then he cocked his head at her. "You're Philander's sister, aren't you?"

She nodded.

"Do ye know him?" She seemed surprised.

"Guess I do," said Gib, and he jumped off the gate. He told her then how Philander had caught Marybell for him the day before, and she laughed and seemed to forget her shyness.

"But Marybell *was* winning, if only . . . Well, she got scared, I guess." Then he added quickly, "My name's Gib."

The girl nodded, "I know. Your pa's Doctor Sylvester Martindale."

"How did you know that?"

"Oh, I reckon most everybody knows," she said.

Gib knew well enough that his father was important in the village, but the girl's mother had known that too, he supposed, and it didn't make her very friendly.

The girl was looking at him gravely. Suddenly she was shy again. "I can't tell ye my own name," she said.

"Why not? I was going to ask."

"Cos it ain't like any other name I've heard."

"I'm sure I'll like it," said Gib quickly.

"I kin write it down for ye. Philander showed me how."

"You mean you know how to write?" He knew she never went to school.

"I'd like to," she said wistfully. "But I kin only do my name like Philander showed me."

"I'd like to see then."

"Ye got a knife?" she asked.

Gib did have a small knife, which he kept fastened to his belt. She took it in both hands and walked to the gate. As he watched, she slowly carved out the letters: D-J-U-L-I-H.

Gib read it through uncertainly. It was indeed

strange to him. Seeing him hesitate she laughed suddenly. "It's Djulih!" She pronounced it *Joolee*. Although when she said it an *h* came on the end of it like a breath. "It's an Injun name," she added. "Me ma named me that, being she's most Injun."

"It's a pretty name," he said.

Djulih picked up one of his baskets. "I kin show ye where puddin' grass grows for cramps," she said. "And wormwood and old man and mugwort. That's good for colds. And lots of others. Come."

Gib was delighted to have his searching made so easy. She showed him where all the herbs were growing. She knew them all, and knew where they grew.

All her shyness seemed to disappear as she ran joyously from place to place, helping to fill up Gib's baskets. By the time the sun began to slide down towards the hills, the baskets were over-flowing with herbs of all kinds. Some Gib had never even heard of, and others Djulih called by different names, like pudding grass for pennyroyal. But Lovina, Gib knew, would receive them all with delight.

They came to the lane some distance below the Perrely house.

"I'll leave you here," Djulih said. He saw that there was a path, which he supposed led around to the back of the house.

"Oh," said Gib surprised; then he hastily added, "I sure thank you for helping me. Lovina's going to be mightily pleased."

Djulih nodded her head solemnly. "Reckon I wouldn't tell no one 'bout me though. Your ma and pa wouldn't like it if'n they was to find out."

"I don't see why," began Gib, but he knew she was right.

"There's reasons, Gib."

"Just because you live in the Hollow . . ."

" 'Tain't the only reason," she said. "You Martindales don't never talk to us Perrelys. My ma's told me."

"But why?"

It was no use. Djulih was gone. Before he could stop her, she had picked up her skirts and run off down the path. He was left standing foolishly in the road with one hand raised as if to hold a flying bird.

Gib moved on rather dejectedly. He hadn't had a chance to ask when he could see her again, or to find out anything about Philander. And the mystery of what seemed to be a feud between their two families was less solved than ever.

As he walked past the Perrely house he stared at it, as if it could reveal the secret to him. Many corners gave it a sense of endless, mysterious space, comfortable quarters for spiders and rats and perhaps ghosts, thought Gib.

How did Pardon Perrely the peddler come to be living in such a house. At one time it must have been quite a grand place. Gib could imagine carriages rolling up before the stone steps, liveried servants holding torches to light the way for elegant men in gay-colored breeches and powdered wigs, their silken, lovely ladies, with rose-petal faces, giggling over the excitement of music coming from the portico. Gib laughed aloud. That was too romantic altogether! But the fact still remained that this was no house for just a peddler, and his Indian wife, no house for people called "low-livin' shiftless . . ." and whatever else the inhabitants of the Hollow were called, as if they were all alike and all of them were to be despised.

The Secret in the Garret

THAT evening Gib's father returned home with deep things on his mind. There had been a town meeting, and as one of the selectmen he had had to argue over the question of a new road going down into the Hollow. Mr. Aaron Coon came to the house, a lean-faced, shrewd-looking man who owned the general store on the green. He was a selectman, and so was Hannibal Sage, the shoemaker, who came with him.

They were sitting about the table in the kitchen, glad of the warmth of the fire; for rain had blown in from the hills and a strange chill had settled about the land.

When the tall imposing parson, the Reverend Elijah

Bownum, arrived with his wife, Gib's mother put aside her sewing and wanted to move to the parlor, as a more fitting place to receive the minister. But Mr. Bownum would have none of it. He sat down at the kitchen table with the others and Mrs. Bownum moved to the corner beside Mrs. Martindale to listen while the men talked.

Granny Hope sat on the settle, as usual so close to the fire she was almost in it. Her eyes peered at the faces of the men, but she held her mouth firmly clenched. Gib kept in the shadows, hoping not to be noticed and sent to bed.

"When they cry for a road," his father was saying, "they don't think of the cost to the village; and they don't consider that a new bridge would have to be built."

"Besides," said the Reverend Mr. Bownum, "what is wrong with the road there already?"

Hannibal Sage peered at the parson, like an inquisitive bird, over the top of his thick glasses. "It is a long journey, Elijah, as it winds now. And the world is getting impatient with long journeys to progress."

Aaron Coon blew air out of his thin cheeks. "We all need to be industrious. But it'll take more'n a straight road to make the Hollow folk amount to a hill of beans."

"Well now," said the shoemaker in his quiet, reasonable voice, "we can't afford to criticize. Things are changin' fast. A lot of us'll be out of business very soon, to let others take over."

Aaron Coon grew impatient. "Philosophy, Hannibal!

All very well in the quiet of your shop, cuttin' leather. But there ain't one family down in the Hollow with enough gumption to take over anythin'."

"Well now, they be clamorin' fur a new road, ain't they?"

"Do I take it, Hannibal," asked Gib's father, "that you're supporting this petition for a new road?"

"I don't say that, no, no. But I'm sayin' it must be thought on. They want to move ahead some. Why even Pardon Perrely was sayin' afore he left . . ."

There was a clamor of protesting voices to drown Hannibal out, and Sylvester Martindale said sternly, "Let us confine ourselves to the question of a new road, not new gossip."

Gib wondered why his father was so worked up.

From the chimney corner the voice of Granny Hope spoke up, as she spat into the fire, "Indifferent, down-right backslidin' heathen reprobates, who've got no call to raise their voices beyond a squeak."

There was a stunned silence. Granny Hope didn't often enter any conversation. She stuck her pipe back into her mouth and stared at the flames as if she could see the heathen burning.

Mr. Bownum looked uneasy. "Why gracious me, Granny Hope, who can you be thinking of?"

But everybody including Gib knew she was talking about the Perrelys.

Granny Hope went on, "It'll never be forgotten, not unless this house was to burn down, an' the garret with all them papers."

"Enough, Granny," snapped Doctor Martindale and slammed the flat of his hand down on the table with such vehemence that the lamp jumped an inch in a great quaver of light.

Granny Hope spat into the fire, and went into a series of subdued mutterings. There was a moment of uneasy silence. Then Doctor Martindale raised his eyes, and Gib found himself trapped by them. "Gibeon."

"Yes, sir," said Gib meekly.

"Go to bed."

Gib turned the words of Granny Hope over and over in his mind. He knew how violent she was whenever her thoughts rested on the Perrelys. But now she had given him something to wonder about. The papers in the garret? What papers? He had been in the garret many times. But where were those papers? There were chests in the garret, both large and small. Gib knew what was in them. His mother had gone up with him once when he was much smaller and let him see inside. There was old finery that used to be worn by the Martindales; his mother's wedding gown. There was a broken faded doll, two cracked mirrors, an old rocking horse, which he used to ride, a wicker cradle that he slept in as a baby. There were many other things of interest to Gib, particularly bits of history such as Grandfather Martindale's sword, the one he had worn while fighting the Red Coats under General Washington. But none of this was what Granny Hope had mentioned.

As Gib was getting into bed and was about to blow out the candle, he remembered that there was one quite large iron chest that he had never looked in. He had tried to open it once, but it seemed to be locked. He wondered where the key was. He wondered and wondered, and fell asleep still wondering.

Lovina had been delighted with the herbs Gib had brought from the Perrely meadows. She asked several times how he had known enough to bring so many of the different kinds of medicine plants, which she called "simples" because she used them for simple remedies. Even Doctor Martindale came to Lovina at times for some of her homemade medicine. She always hung the herbs in the garret to dry out, and then they were ready. The next day, she asked Gib if he would help her carry the herbs into the garret. He jumped at the chance.

Lovina, with a candle in her hand, hoisted her great weight up the creaking wooden stairs that climbed steeply behind the brick of the central chimney. Gib brought the herbs from the kitchen, rushing up the attic stairs in his haste to get there. Lovina soon became lost in the sorting out of herbs ready for hanging.

She was in the west part of the garret, by the small square window, which gave her better light than the candle. The locked iron chest was at the other end. This was Gib's opportunity, and he knew it. He approached the chest, found it locked, but soon realized that one of the hinges at the back was broken. The other hinge was half eaten away by rust. He looked around and found a broken andiron lying beside the wicker cradle. Inserting this behind the hinge, he broke it at little more than a touch.

Lifting the lid carefully for fear it would squeak, he peered in. There seemed to be nothing but clothes, layed out neatly and smelling of camphor. He ran his hand over them. They were silky in feel. There were bits of lace and fancy things. He pulled out one of the garments, a lovely blue velvet, that turned out to be a pair of breeches such as men had worn in the days when the King of England ruled, before long pantaloons came into fashion.

There was a three-cornered hat stuffed in the side of the chest. Gib took it out and placed it on his head. His hands burrowed on, deep into the clothes. Was there nothing in the chest but old finery, just as in the other chests?

Suddenly he felt something else. Papers! He lifted them out. What he had in his hand was a bundle of letters tied around with a ribbon. Letters? They surely wouldn't reveal very much. He tried unsuccessfully to read one without undoing the ribbon, but he didn't feel right about reading other people's letters. He put them back in the chest. Feeling further with his hand, he realized that the bottom of the chest had several layers of papers. This time when he drew his hand out, he was holding a bunch of yellow-leafed documents. He started to read, but the tiny spidery writing was almost

impossible to make out in the dim garret light. He was just putting all the papers back when his eye caught a line of words on one that made him start. He pulled that document out and slid it gently into his shirt front, hoping he could find a way to put it back later.

It was at that moment that Lovina chose to turn around. "Master Gib! Lord o' mercy, what are ye up to there!" She came thundering down on him. "And what you got on your head?"

"Nothing," said Gib quickly. "Just an old hat."

"Nothing! Why, that's from the chest. Look at them things!"

She had stopped in the midst of what was about to be a tirade. Her eyes bulged at the elegant clothes and fine laces exposed to the light of the candle in her hand. Gib was relieved to see that she had not discovered the document he had put in his shirt.

"Just old clothes," he said.

"Well now, ye'd better close it down, afore yer pa hears about what ye're up to."

"Nothing of importance," said Gib as he tossed the hat back and closed the lid down.

"Now, Gib, you come and help me. Idle fingers make mischief, sure enough."

It was not until nightfall that Gib was able to look at his captured treasure in safety. Earlier than usual in the evening, he stopped to light a taper for his candle.

"Stop playin' with fire," muttered Granny Hope.

"I'm only going to bed," said Gib. He saw his mother

looking at him and quickly made the excuse of being tired. His father was too busy with his accounts in the next room to concern himself with his son's condition.

Lydia Martindale laid her sewing down as Gib approached. She put her pale, always cool, hand up to his forehead as if she thought he had a fever.

"Are you well, Gib?"

"Yes, Mother, quite well thank you."

"What's this bruise on your arm?"

"It's nothing, Mother. I just fell."

From the chimney corner came the cracked voice of Granny Hope, "It is not the business of a Martindale to fall!"

His mother turned in one of her rare moments of spirit, "Oh, Granny Hope, Gib is only a boy!"

"Go to bed, Gibeon." It was the stern voice of his father who was bothered by the conversation; he could not concentrate. Gib pulled quickly away from his mother and scrambled up the stairs to the privacy of his room, holding his hand to his chest to reassure himself that the precious parchment was still there.

Gib pulled the document out of his shirt and tucked it under his pillow until he got undressed and into his bed. Then, his hand trembling with excitement, he drew the document out to read. He had reason to believe that some of the mystery of the Perrely's would be solved for him, for in the garret his eye had caught part of a sentence. It read: "To my erstwhile son, Philander Perrely Martindale . . ." *Erstwhile,* he knew, meant something like *Once upon a time, but not now.*

There it was now, standing out in the tiny delicate hand of the legal document, surrounded with phrases like "whereas the aforementioned" and so on. All these strange phrases made the whole thing very difficult for Gib to grasp. Added to this difficulty was the fact that much of the parchment was faded with age, for it was dated "the sixteenth of February, the Year of Our Lord, 1702."

The candle by Gib's bed had quite drowned in its own grease by the time he had grasped what was being said. The document was a will made out by one who had the same name as Gib's father—Sylvester Martindale, and on the top of the parchment had been written "Property of Sylvester Martindale Esquire." There was a great deal about the parceling out of moneys and goods and lands. It was certain that this Martindale must have had considerable wealth when he died.

The part that interested Gib more than all the rest was the section dealing with the son, Philander Perrely Martindale, who was for some reason disgraced and was to be regarded as a true son no longer. He was to be cut off from the family without a penny. But he was to be given a house beyond the Quinebaug to live in without rent as long as he paid the taxes. Before his death he would have the right to buy the house if he could for seven hundred pounds English money. There followed some pious phrases which said that Philander Perrely Martindale would have the chance to redeem himself before the eyes of the Lord by earning his living in some honest labor.

If he failed to buy the house before his death, the estate would be taken away from his heirs. Apart from this house, he would get nothing. Everything else would go to his brother, Gibeon Sylvester Martindale, and the two brothers were to have no more to say to each other for the rest of their days on earth.

Gibeon—that was his own name! How strange that his name should be so disastrously coupled with the name of Philander! Well, at least the first Philander must have done well enough to buy the house, since the Perrelys still lived in it. Providing, of course, the peddler Pardon Perrely was directly descended from this disgraced Martindale brother. If so, Gib reasoned, the Martindales and the Perrelys were related, and Philander and Djulih were actually Gib's cousins, though several times removed by the passing of generations.

The thought so excited Gib that he could hardly sleep that night, and when he did, it was to dream of wars and bloody feuds between members of the two families, and of Philander Perrely grimly moving toward him with his primed gun.

The next day Gib chopped and sawed wood like a madman, determined to escape before the morning was half over. His father had told him to take the small farm cart by late afternoon across the river to where the neighbors were helping in the apple orchard of Willis

Pickle's father. Gib's plan was to rush off early and so have some time before he would have to put in an appearance at the orchard. He wanted to find his new friend Djulih, perhaps his cousin, and tell her the news.

How he was going to find her, he did not know, when he started out. He certainly could not go to the Perrely house openly, with Djulih's mother so hostile. He would have to tether Marybell somewhere unseen and do some clever scouting on Perrely land.

As a first step, he tied Marybell out in a meadow, where she and the cart were concealed from the road behind a high hedge. He then began a stealthy circuit around the old house. There was no sign of life. He crept a little nearer, feeling very daring.

Nothing happened, so he grew steadily bolder. It was easy to approach the house by stages because there were so many old weather-beaten wooden structures about the yard. He moved from one to another.

At the back of a rather large barn he paused, peering round at the house, now quite near to him. He had begun to ask himself what he intended to do, when he was startled by a voice almost at his shoulder.

"Them hats I made more of, 'cos ye said ye could sell 'em."

Gib realized the words were coming from inside the barn, and that it was the voice of Mrs. Perrely.

A man's voice answered. "So I will in time, I reckon." That was Aaron Coon, who owned the general store in the village.

"But we need the food bad, Mr. Coon. I'm tellin' ye." Djulih's mother seemed quite upset.

"Don't the peddler keep you proper?"

"Reckon ye know Mr. Perrely's away. Been away months already. Can't tell when he'll be back neither. Most like we'll starve afore then."

"Well, Ma'am," said Aaron Coon, "can't find no way to trade them palm hats quicker than I can. As it is, I got ye the palm leaves without askin' nothin' for 'em."

"But if ye could see your way to givin' me somethin' now. We need food bad."

Mr. Coon cut her off. "Can't see my way that way at all. Can't give ye nothin' till I sell the lot of 'em. I don't calculate to lose any on speculation. I'm a sober man, Ma'am. I got me pride and me reputation, ye might say. And hain't got no call to alter any."

Gib started to move away, afraid they might come out of the barn, but in his haste he tripped over a cracked plow handle that lay hidden in the weeds, and he fell.

Aaron Coon's voice came to a sudden stop. Then he asked sharply, "What was that? You got stray cattle here? 'Cos if that be someone nosing around . . ."

Gib did not stay to hear more. He picked himself up and lunged off to hide.

He waited some minutes. Nothing happened, so he decided it would be wise to move off. The only problem was that to get back to the road, he was obliged to cross the lane leading up to the Perrely house. As he was doing so, he saw Aaron Coon. It was too late to hide himself a second time. Mr. Coon was as surprised by the meeting as he was.

His expression of surprise changed quickly to anger, and he shouted, "What are ye snoopin' around here fur, Gib Martindale? Ye know your pa's goin' to lick the hide off'n ye for comin' near the Perrelys."

"I was just on my way to Mr. Pickle's orchard . . ." Gib said lamely.

"This ain't Pickle's orchard. Now ye git off'n this place afore I cause trouble."

"Yes, Mr. Coon."

Gib was worried. If Aaron Coon did tell his father, punishment was sure; but what was worse, he would most likely be given orders never to come this way again.

He had started across the meadow towards the old farm gate and was passing under a tree when he jumped in sudden terror. His ears rang as he flattened himself to the ground. A shot—it could only have been from a gun—had struck across the silence and echoed in the valley. A small branch, for no apparent reason, dropped downwards, striking him on the back.

Gib waited, peering around him. Was it Aaron Coon chasing him with a gun? Surely that couldn't be. He lifted himself up. As he did so, he saw a movement about one hundred and fifty yards away. A man holding a gun stood in plain view. Gib was about to turn and run, when he saw, that it was Philander Perrely.

His first thought was that Philander, too, was hunting him off the land, but he changed his mind when he saw that Philander was waving a hand at him. It was like a greeting. It certainly wasn't anger. Then Philander laughed, quite distinctly, and vanished into the underbrush.

Djulih's Despair

GIB stood where he was for quite a long time in uncertainty. He half expected Philander to appear in some unlikely fashion, like magic, up out of the ground. But there was only silence, until he heard the sound of Aaron Coon's cart moving slowly along the road above, evidently on the way back into town.

Uneasily, Gib started on towards the farm gate. He could not go back toward the Perrely house now, with Philander prowling about like a savage Indian in the underbrush, wildly shooting off his gun!

Gib smiled to himself. Was it wild shooting? The ball from Philander's rifle had struck the branch above

42

Gib's head so that it fell on Gib's back. Was Philander so sure of his aim that he had done it on purpose? If so, then Philander's marksmanship was much better than rumored in the village.

Gib approached the gate and started to lift himself up, but first he paused and looked around. He was getting jumpy. He put one foot up on the rail, and then he heard his name called.

"Gib."

It was the soft, shy voice of Djulih. She stood staring at him from the same place he had first met her. This time she had on a purple dress that went well with her dark hair, though Gib could see the dress was far from new. It made her look quite dressed up despite her lack of shoes.

"Oh, good morning," said Gib. "I'm glad I found you." He smiled at her with deep relief. If they had not met each other there at the gate, he thought, they might never have met again.

"Have ye been lookin' for me then?"

He leaned on the gate and nodded. Djulih glanced at him, then she looked down at her feet stroking the grass blades with her toes. It occurred to Gib that she looked rather sad. Had something happened he didn't know about?

"Your brother just shot at me with his gun," he said, and watched for her reaction.

But she did not look up at all. "He's allus doin' that. He once knocked a hat off'n my head."

"Shot it off! With his gun!" Gib exclaimed in horror. Perhaps she was joking.

"It was an old hat. Didn't much matter." She looked up at him, and as their eyes met, they both burst out laughing. Then she added, "But he never should've done it to you."

"Oh, that's all right," Gib said off-handedly, as he climbed over the gate to her side.

"When I see'd ye headin' this way, I come to meet you."

"I'm glad you did," said Gib, suddenly remembering the document and putting his hand to his shirt to feel if it was safe.

But she went on, " 'cos I have to be sayin' good-by soon, an' I thought I might not be seein' ye again 'fore I go."

Before Gib could think about it, his hand was clutching her arm, "Djulih, what do you mean?"

She kept her eyes down and seemed suddenly shy again. She did not speak at once.

He took his hand away. "But where are you going, Djulih?"

She turned abruptly away and began to walk slowly along what looked to Gib like a cattle path or a deer path leading through a new growth of trees and clumps of high bramble. Gib hurried to move up beside her. He found that she was crying, for she sniffed repeatedly and rubbed her cheeks with her sleeve. He didn't know what to say.

They had come out on a meadow which sloped sharply. She moved downwards, quickening her pace, as she almost had to do. Gib followed, feeling rather desperate.

At the bottom of the slope was a brook, sparkling in the sun and making a constant tinkling sound over the pebbles on the clear shallow bottom. Here, on the bank, she sat down and slowly slid her toes into the water. She had stopped crying, and even smiled down at her toes. Gib stuck his own feet in the water beside hers. It felt cool and fresh. It made him want to splash, but he kept his feet still as Djulih started to speak again.

"It's partly the reason Mr. Coon come visitin'. He's fixin' it up so I kin work at the mill over to Lowell."

"Mill!" Gib was dismayed.

"It's Mr. Lowell's spinnin' mill, most forty miles east of here. He do take in girls at a dollar a week and the bed an' board is free."

"And you would go and live there, away from home?"

Gib realized that was a foolish thing to say before he had it half out of his mouth. Her tears began to flow again, and she turned her head away.

"I've got something to show you, Djulih. It's very important."

She caught the sudden excitement in his voice, and she half turned to him, sniffing back her tears impatiently.

"What is it, Gib?"

"Do you know, Djulih," he said. "You may turn out

to be my cousin."

She looked full at him then, her eyes wide, her black lashes shining with the damp of vanished tears. He pulled out the document.

"Look at this. I found it in our garret. It was in a chest amongst a lot of old-time finery and three-cornered hats and breeches and lace and things." He held the document out for her to see.

"What is it?" she asked. "What does it say? Can ye read it, Gib?"

"Of course." He didn't speak of the number of hours it had taken him to do it. "Would *you* like to learn to read, Djulih?"

"Oh, I would."

"Maybe I can teach you."

"Oh yes. I'd like to go to school, too. But what's the paper say?"

He told her what he'd read, and she listened with wide unblinking eyes. Her mouth was half open, as if her wonder at his story had driven her breath away.

"So you see," he said at last, "if you go back far enough, we both had the same ancestor. That'd be the father of those two brothers, Philander Perrely Martindale and Gibeon Sylvester Martindale. That means you, Djulih, are a Martindale, too."

Djulih blinked suddenly and clapped her hands over her cheeks, "Really, Gib, really?"

She looked so comical that Gib started to laugh. She stared a moment, then joined in until they were both

rolling on the bank like a couple of puppies.

It took them a little while to get serious, then Djulih began to wonder. "But that Philander Perrely Martindale sort o' dropped part of his name, didn't he?"

"I reckon," said Gib, "he didn't want to think any more about the Martindale part."

"I wonder what he'd done."

"Married an Indian woman, maybe." He said that without thinking. He glanced at Djulih to see if he had offended her, but she nodded her head seriously.

"That's what my pa's done," she said, "for my ma's most Algonquin."

"I heard your mother in the barn, Djulih. She's trying to sell palm hats to Mr. Coon."

"Yes." Djulih nodded gloomily. "But he won't pay us afore he's sold the lot."

"But what about your father? Won't he come back soon?"

Djulih shrugged. "Mebbe he'll come back soon. But mebbe he won't have no money nor food on him. He gets to paintin' so much he forgets to sell what's in the cart."

"Painting?"

"Makin' pictures."

"What sort of pictures, Djulih?"

"With colors an' everything. An' puts pretty frames around 'em too."

"Oh," cried Gib astonished, "he makes pictures with brushes and paints!"

Djulih nodded. She looked at Gib rather shyly, as if afraid he would laugh. But he didn't. He tried to imagine Pardon Perrely sitting in a meadow painting a picture. But then, he thought, why should he be surprised? He really did not know her father well enough to question her story.

He folded the document carefully. "Do you think your father knows about this?"

She shook her head. "I can't justly say. He's never spoke about it to me."

"You should stay in Sturbridge, Djulih," said Gib with a sudden burst of enthusiasm. "Together, maybe, we could put an end to this family feuding."

"How?"

But Gib had no plan.

Djulih added forlornly, "Besides we need the money I can bring back."

"A dollar a week's not much for a family."

"Ain't no way as I kin make more at the mill, with me only twelve."

Then he was right, Gib thought. She was the same age as he was.

"Why doesn't Philander work?" he asked.

She turned on him, her eyes flashing. "If it warn't for Philander's fishin' and huntin' we'd most starve."

Gib liked the way she defended her brother, and he said quickly, "I guess that's so. I wasn't meaning to criticize, Djulih."

"He worked in the mill hisself oncet," she said. "But

the manager took his job away from him."

"What for?"

"He found Philander takin' one o' the spinnin' frames apart."

Gib laughed. "What was he doing that for?"

"Said he wanted to test his idea of a mule that worked by itself."

"A what?"

"I remember that's what he said."

"But what does it mean, Djulih?"

"I an't just capable to say. Somethin' on the machine."

"It sounds like an improvement, if it worked."

"The manager didn't want no improvement. Philander don't talk about it now. But he's allus inventin' things."

The more Gib heard about Philander, the more he decided he liked him. He wished he could get someone to help, for he figured that Philander needed money to get his inventions on the market. But first there was Djulih. Perhaps she could get some work in the village instead of going away.

He put the question to her, but Djulih shook her head. "I asked Mr. Coon 'bout that. He says there ain't nothin'. But I suspicion it's 'cos nobody'll trust me, 'count o' me bein' a Perrely. But I kin cook, an' I kin sew, an' I kin keep house, too. I kin do most all there's to do in a house. But they don't want me 'cos I'm a Perrely, an' my ma's a Injun."

Later, while Gib was working in Mr. Pickle's orchard, he tried to think of something he could do to keep Djulih from going away. He was afraid to talk to his father about it, knowing how his father felt about the Perrelys. His mother would only become frightened of trouble. His mother, he decided, always wanted everything to remain the way it was, undisturbed.

There was still no solution to the problem the next morning. But Gib was still working on it. It was Sunday morning. Sundays were very special days in Sturbridge. It was the Sabbath day, the Lord's day, the day of rest, which meant that nobody would do any work. It was a day when no activity went on in the house or around the house: no farming, beyond the feeding and watering of animals, no wood-chopping or gardening for Gib, no spinning or sewing or knitting for his mother, no house-work or even cooking for Lovina. Sabbath was the day most of the families of the community ate baked beans and brown bread, Indian pudding and pies, all of which had been prepared on Saturday night. Lovina would put the beans in the brick oven and leave them to bake over night.

In the early morning, all was concentrated on getting ready before the church bell started ringing, and getting into the church before it stopped. Gib liked the Sabbath mornings when everything was still, not a soul out on the streets or on the green or on the roads beyond the village or out in the meadows or in the woods. It was a world of strange quiet, almost as if a spell had been cast over the land. He could see this enchanted world from his bedroom window. This morning he let his gaze go out across the valley. He could see a tip of Farmer Petit's barn, and below that a bit of the covered bridge, but there were too many trees to see anything of the Perrely house in the Hollow.

He wondered how the Sabbath was kept by the Perrelys. He guessed, since none of them ever came to Sunday meeting, that the day was no different for them from any other day.

Hearing activity beginning downstairs, Gib realized he was dreaming and hurriedly finished his dressing. Yet his mind kept wandering off, thinking of the Perrelys: Philander, unable to get anywhere with his inventions; Mrs. Perrely, lonely and resentful against the world; and most of all Djulih, about to set off alone to work in a mill miles and miles away, to be among strangers, with no family and no home.

The meeting house was set on a knoll at the west end of the village green, overlooking the village. On Sabbath mornings, most of the families who lived anywhere near left their carts and carriages at home and walked to the meeting. It was a very solemn parade, for this was not considered a time for gossip. Conversation was rare, beyond the morning greeting of neighbor to neighbor. The solemnity of the occasion was begun by Elijah Bownum himself, who made it a point to stroll alone about the green long before the meeting house bell began its summoning. Tall and gaunt, dressed in black, with his gold-headed cane as his symbol of authority, he presented a forbidding picture. It was as though he thought perpetually of the sternness of God's law.

As the bell of the meeting house began to toll, he would disappear between the high white Doric pillars. And all the neighbors lucky enough to be ready on time would come out of their doors and begin the slow stroll toward the glistening white steepled building.

Granny Hope always walked just behind Gib's father and mother; and as long as Gib could remember, he had walked behind his grandmother, and Lovina just behind him. Families with many children presented an even more impressive picture, with the children stretched out in a long line from the oldest to the youngest, with perhaps a maiden aunt bringing up the rear.

The meeting house had a gallery on three sides. Up the uncarpeted wooden stairs went the boys in their best squeaky boots, Gib included. They would sit in the gallery on either side. The singers were in the gallery, too, but facing the pulpit. Up there, it was very conspicuous and not a good place for open misbehavior.

The sternness of Elijah Bownum became instead shining fire when he presented himself at the pulpit. The fire enlivened his lean body and shone in his eyes. His frown became expressive; his smile flashed. He stirred up the air with a flowering of energy. His Sabbath sermons were not to be forgotten easily.

Gib wondered whether he would be able to concentrate this morning. His head was filled with the problem of the Perrelys. Gradually, however, the magic of Mr. Bownum's sermon enticed him out of his broodings, until he was soon carried off into thoughts on the perpetual warmth of God's love for man and the need for neighbor to love neighbor. It suddenly made Gib aware that this was the very thing that was not going on between the Martindales and the Perrelys. He looked down at his father's profile to see if he was absorbing the message fully.

Sylvester Martindale sat stiffly upright against the closed-in family pew, with Lydia Martindale and Granny Hope Martindale on either side of him, and Lovina bulging over the pew door. It was not easy to decide at any time what Doctor Martindale was thinking, for he kept his face stern. He always looked dignified and intelligent. Most men seemed to look up to him. This served very well for the community doctor upon whose decisions so many depended.

But for the success of a plan Gib had finally worked out, he had to reach in his father some inner quality of kindness. He decided to make use of Mr. Bownum's sermon as a beginning. Gib knew he would not be able to talk to his father that day. On the Sabbath, conversation was rather strictly held down to religious questions. He would approach his father the following day, Monday, during the midday meal.

A Battle Begins

GIB was a little disturbed when he found that the parson and the parson's wife had been invited to dine with the Martindales the next day. In the presence of company, it was not thought proper for a child to talk very much. Even Gib's mother would be unusually silent, and Mrs. Bownum always listened so attentively to the words of her husband that she had no words of her own.

He kept very silent at first and watched his manners at the table so that his father would be pleased with him. He saw his father's eyebrows raise when his son rushed to help Lovina carry plates from the kitchen. This was a sign of approval.

55

Even Granny Hope was served remarkably well by Gib. She forgot to condemn the coming generation as "sinfully lazy," and patted him on the cheek when he brought her her tobacco pouch. She then retired to her corner inside the kitchen fireplace for she "never did take to green apple pies" and preferred to suck on her pipe.

Over the pie, Gib listened to his father "talking government." Gib was grateful that in spite of the subject his father was in a good mood. Government talk more often aroused complaints and stern predictions. But the selectmen of Sturbridge had succeeded in putting off the request for a new road.

When the winter snows came, the valley people would suffer, Gib supposed. Anyhow his father was enjoying his triumph, and even Elijah Bownum smiled contentedly.

Sylvester Martindale made a jest, "You can have all your neighbor-love-neighbor up in the pulpit, Elijah; but when it comes to town government, reason and plain good sense must always come first."

Gib's mother was shocked. "Why, Sylvester, you hadn't ought to speak like that, even in fun!" she exclaimed; and with cheeks flaming, she worried at her pie with a spoon.

The parson laughed. He welcomed this sort of thing. "Loving your neighbor, Sylvester, doesn't go contrary to plain good sense. It goes right along with it."

Gib's father tossed his head back and laughed too.

"I'd say," the parson went on, "that most of us stubborn Yankees have got a lot more to learn about neighbor-loving."

"I think," spoke up Mrs. Martindale again, with unusual forcefulness, "that your Sabbath sermon, Mr. Bownum, was uncommon fine."

"Thank you, Mrs. Martindale. Thank you."

Gib's mother had not finished. "And I think folks would be a lot happier if they did think a little more kindly of other people in everyday ordinary things."

"What sort of things, Lydia?" asked Gib's father somewhat heavily.

"Oh, I don't know . . . everyday little things . . ." She hesitated and looked pleadingly at Mr. Bownum, who nodded his head but left her to her fate.

"My wife is one of these radicals, Parson. Because we trounced the King and his royalists in two displays of violence, she thinks the whole of life should be turned upside-down and shaken."

"Oh no, Sylvester," protested Mrs. Martindale in distress, "I didn't say that."

"Thought it," came the voice of Granny Hope from the kitchen corner, for she hadn't been missing a word.

"There's something to say for the old days, just the same," insisted Mr. Martindale, "when folks possessed a sense of duty. If they did wrong, they came to the church to plead for forgiveness. Nowadays, folks do wrong and dare the church to raise as much as a shocked finger."

"It's the unforgiving nature of the Yankee heart that has to be dealt with first," said the parson.

Gib's father made a sound of disgust.

"No, no, Sylvester," said the parson. "To forgive is oftentimes to heal. Try it. We should all try it. All here should try it."

Gib could hear Granny Hope as she spat loudly into the fire. Then he heard his own voice speaking into the silence. It hardly seemed his own, for he found himself as frightened as a raw recruit going into battle. "Could I try it too, Mr. Bownum, sir?"

His father frowned, but the parson looked at Gib in amazement, then smiled with his thin lips.

"Sure thing, Gib," he said. "But who is there for you to forgive?"

"Well sir, when grown-ups won't forgive some folks who I feel ought to be forgiven, should I forgive, even if . . ." Gib stopped, amazed that he had been able to get that far.

"Even if what, son?" his father pressed ominously.

"Even if . . . if my parents disapproved, sir," said Gib in a rush.

"Gibeon, what does this mean?" asked his father.

His mother looked frightened. "Gib, you know you should never interrupt your father . . ."

But Doctor Martindale cut her off. "Lydia, if our son has something to say, let him say it."

"Ah yes," said Mr. Bownum, "in a true republic even the sons can speak up to their fathers, eh, Gib?"

Gib swallowed hard. "I mean, I was thinking in church what Mr. Bownum said . . ."

"Well, what about it? Speak up, boy." His father was not giving him much time.

"Well, I was trying to think who I could be good to. I mean, that is, someone I wouldn't be good to in an ordinary way."

"Go on."

"But that is well and fine," interrupted the parson. "There is hope for the world if the young ones consider such things.

"Go on, son."

"I was wondering about the poor folk in the valley." Now it was out.

"Oh," said Mr. Bownum somewhat uncomfortable.

"There now!" croaked Granny Hope like doom from around the corner.

"But don't they have to be loved, too, like neighbors?" pleaded Gib, losing heart.

His father scraped his chair back from the table. "It is always dangerous to pour mature wisdom into the ears of babes," he said sternly. "Parson Bownum, you have something to answer for."

This was greeted by an uneasy silence. Mr. Martindale turned to Gib. "Get up, boy," he said, "and come here."

"Sylvester, now," cried his mother.

Gib rose from the table and approached his father, whose face was pale with rage.

"Now face the table, Gibeon, and give a proper account of yourself. You've been trespassing on the lands of the peddler, Pardon Perrely. Is that not so?"

Gib's heart sank. Aaron Coon had told his father after all. "Yes, sir," Gib said.

"To trespass without permission on another's property is a sin," his father went on. "Is this the way to love your neighbor?"

"I was only . . ."

His father cut him off. "To stare into your neighbor's windows and listen behind doors is a sin again. I had thought to let the matter rest without speaking of it, but I see you are quite without repentence."

Gib was so stunned by his father's severity that he could find no words to speak in his own defense.

Mr. Bownum coughed uneasily, and began, "Perhaps, Sylvester, we should not judge too severely . . ."

But Gib's father stopped him with a gesture. "Go to your room, boy, and stay there until I come up."

Gib knew there was nothing he could say when his father spoke in this manner. With his face burning with frustration, Gib turned, moved out of the room, and climbed the stairs.

He didn't know how the conversation went on after that, for no one spoke until he had closed his door. He went to his bed and sat down limply.

He thought of Djulih. He had intended to help her, but he had certainly made a mess of things.

His father had said he would come up. Gib expected

he would be punished. The worst punishment would be the forbidding of any more visits into the valley. He might never see Philander again. He would not even be able to explain to Djulih why he did not see her any more. He had arranged to meet her the next day, Tuesday afternoon, by the old farm gate. She would go there expecting to see him, hoping for good news. Instead, she would wait, perhaps hours, until all hope had vanished. What would she think of him?

He grew desperate at the thought. He kept listening for the sound of his father's steps ascending the stairs, but they did not come. It was as if he had been forgotten altogether. This was worse than punishment to Gib. But there was always work to be done around the house and on the farm. Gib's eventual punishment would probably mean the cutting off of free time until school opened. He would be set to work afternoons as well as mornings, with no rest until dark.

Still nothing happened. The Reverend Elijah Bownum and his wife left. Gib saw them from the window beside his bed. Then he saw his father. He came out of the door and stood for a short time gazing silently over the green, leaning against the white picket fence. Finally he turned and entered the house again. Gib thought his father would come then, up the stairs, and he prepared for the scolding he would get. But no footsteps climbed the stairs.

It was late afternoon before Gib had any sense of belonging to the family again. The stairs began to creak loudly as they always did when Lovina came up. Gib hurried to the door and flung it open as soon as Lovina's knuckles touched the panel.

"Lovina, I'm glad to see you . . . somebody . . ." he began, but Lovina frowned and put her finger to her lips. Carrying a small tray, she came in and closed the door.

"I don't know what ye've done, Gib, but certain 'tis your pa's right vexed, an' won't even talk to nobody."

"But, Lovina, isn't he coming up to me? He said he would."

"Better he don't then, for storm's brewin' in his face all afternoon."

Lovina set the tray on a table beside Gib's bed. "Mrs. Martindale tol' me to fetch ye this, 'gainst ye was gettin' hungry. Seems awful concerned 'bout ye. What've ye done, now, Gib?"

"I only went on the Perrely land, looking for Djulih."

Lovina screwed up her face as if she had been struck. "Pardon Perrely's girl! What call ye got lookin' fur that one?"

"What's wrong with it?"

"But nobody speaks to them Perrelys, save maybe it's to the peddler when it's fur buyin' offn his cart."

"Well, Aaron Coon does, because I saw him there. In fact, it was Mr. Coon who went and told my father."

But Lovina didn't know anything about that. She only repeated, "Nothin' good comes of Perrelys."

"You got your herbs, Lovina, anyway," Gib said

mischievously.

Lovina's mouth dropped open. She even felt for a chair to give her support, and she sank down on it. "You mean you got them simples from that black Injun, Pardon Perrely's woman?"

"Djulih showed me where they grew and helped me pick them."

"The little witch!" cried Lovina. "If I'd a-known!"

"I don't see why the Perrelys should be thought so bad," began Gib getting worked up. "Nobody believes that stuff about witches any more. There's something else back of it, and I think I know what it is."

"Gib now, han't ye done enough!" Lovina had been in the house too long not to know something of Gib's stubbornness as soon as he got an idea in his head. And it was clear now that he did not mean to be put off.

"Lovina," he said, "please do something for me now. Take something to my mother. It's very important. You don't have to say anything. Just give this to her when she's alone and say it's from me."

"What is it, Gib?" asked Lovina as she stared suspiciously at the yellowed pages.

"Just an old document I found."

Gib knew he was taking a chance, that his mother might show it to his father, that it would all come out about how he had stolen it from the chest in the garret. But he did not care. He could not go on pretending he did not know.

The Disastrous Adventure

LOVINA had gone down with the document tucked in the front of her dress, grumbling as she went. But deep down, Gib could see, she was driven by curiosity about the papers, which were too complicated for her to decipher with her little knowledge of reading. Lovina might protest over pleasing Gib at any time, but she would usually end up by doing as he asked. That knowledge was a kind of bond between them.

It was not long before Gib's patience was rewarded by the sound of his mother coming up the stairs. She pushed the door open and came in. Gib could see at once that she looked pale and frightened. She pressed the door to, and leaned against it with her eyes closed, as if faint.

Gib got up to go to her, "What is it, mother? Are you unwell?"

She opened her eyes at the concern in his voice, and let her thin delicate hand run down the back of his head. Then she crossed to his bed and sat down.

"Gib, where did you get this?" She held the document out towards him.

He told her about the chest in the garret. "I know, it was wrong of me to look in there," he said. "But you see, I did and I know all about it now."

Mrs. Martindale sighed. "I suppose so," she said. "But your father . . ." Then she stopped as if the weight of decision was too much for her. For a moment she put her hands up to her face and looked as if she were going to weep. But she pulled herself together, and didn't.

"Sit down, Gib," she said, patting the bed beside her. "We shall have to talk now."

He sat beside her, but when she said nothing more, he asked her why his father had not come up as he had said he would.

"Your father is deeply moved," she said. "There was talk after you left, Gib. Mr. Bownum was touched by your words. The things he said were not lost on your father."

"Isn't he going to punish me then?"

"I don't know, Gib. He's never acted this way

before. I can't rightly say what he'll do."

Gib stroked the document with his finger and looked gravely up into his mother's face. "This means Mr. Perrely and us Martindales are related doesn't it, mother?"

"Yes, Gib."

"Then why do we hate each other?"

"Hate?" His mother clutched the beads around her neck as if distressed, but she added quickly, "Yes, Gib. That is what it is, isn't it? What do you think we should do?"

Gib eyed his mother sharply. It was the first time he could remember that she had consulted him in this way. It made him feel important, grown-up, and strangely purposeful.

"We could help Djulih Perrely, Mother."

"Is that the daughter?"

"Yes. You see, they need help. They can't live unless Djulih works. Mr. Coon is getting her a job in a spinning mill. She'll have to go miles away from home and live with strangers, and all for only one dollar a week."

"But how do you know all about this, Gib?"

Mrs. Martindale listened astonished while Gib told her the details of his meetings with Djulih. When he saw how sympathetic she was, he rushed out with his plan. "Couldn't we give her work here, Mother? She could help Lovina. She knows how to cook and everything, and she's very nice."

Mrs. Martindale smiled fleetingly, then closed her eyes and turned her face away.

"What did that Philander Perrely Martindale do, Mother, a hundred and thirty-two years ago that was so terrible?"

"Granny Hope knows, Gib. She told me."

"What was it?"

"He needed money to pay off debts, and so he stole something from his father—something very valuable, it was. His father had him arrested, and he spent some time in jail."

"In jail!"

"Yes, his own father put him there. Then he took to drinking rum and barely made a living. He refused to use the Martindale name and had it changed to Perrely, and the village turned against him . . . and every one of the Perrelys ever since."

Lydia looked at Gib quickly and added, "Oh, I don't say it's right. But you see how your father is. What can I do?"

"I wasn't trespassing on Mr. Perrely's land," said Gib suddenly. "I was looking for Djulih, who's my friend."

"If your father thinks that Djulih is your friend, he'll be more angry than before."

"I think that's stupid," burst out Gib.

Lydia stood up in horror and said faintly, "Gib, Gib!"

He got to his feet and faced her, about to say more, but he managed to keep it back. "I'm sorry, Mother."

She sighed and put a hand on his shoulder. "Gib, you have the spirit of a Martindale already, almost a man at that." Then she turned and move to the door. "I will try to speak to your father. But have a little patience, Gib."

"Yes, mother."

He heard her going down the stairs, and then there was silence. The silence continued into the evening.

Gib had gotten himself into bed for the night when he heard his father's tread on the stairs. He waited, his pulse pounding, hardly able to breathe, but his father did not stop at his door. Gib heard him going into his room. Soon he heard his mother hurrying up after her husband. Then the door closed, and there was silence.

Gib tried to go to sleep. This was hard, for his mind kept worrying over the events of the day just past and the possible events of the day to come.

He got out of bed at last and padded across the room to peer out of the window. The moon was full. The pale landscape looked mysterious and still, a place of ghosts. He wished he could go out. He supposed a ghost would frighten him, but he would very much like to see one. He looked below the window and measured the distance to the ground. It was not too far to jump he supposed, since his feet would land on the grass below. But he didn't; and when he got back to bed, he fell asleep almost at once.

The next morning, no one came to visit him but Lovina, who grumbled loudly about having to carry his meals up and down the stairs when she had too much to do in the kitchen already. It seemed that both his father and mother had left the house together in the chaise, the fast one-horse cart that his father used when visiting his patients. He hadn't seen them go, for the barn was on the other side of the house. It was not unusual for his mother to go with his father, but Gib felt resentful that she had not tried to see him before she left.

"What am I supposed to do?" he grumbled. "Stay here all day?"

But Lovina knew nothing. "If your father says to stay in your room, then you stay in your room or there'll be a storm o' trouble. It be none of my doin'.'"

By the afternoon, when his parents did not return, Gib had had enough. Perhaps if he sneaked out of the house without anyone seeing him, he could run down to the valley by the shortcut through the woods, find Djulih, and be back before anyone found out he had left his room.

He opened his door and listened. He could hear Lovina moving about. She was cleaning the sitting room. It was obvious he could not get down the stairs without her seeing him. He went back to the window and studied the ground. He could catch a branch of the bush that almost reached his window and that would check his fall. He closed his door and bolted it, then crossed to the window and climbed out.

He was in such a hurry that he almost slipped. It came as a warning for more caution. Looking quickly, toward the green, he saw that there was no one near.

He caught the branch, dropped, and came down sprawling, but unhurt. No one was about, so no one had seen him. Racing at once to the back of the house, he ducked behind the bushes. There he was safe and could get away unseen. He started across the meadow toward the woods.

There was one farmhouse he had to pass going down that way, old Orasmus Petit's house. If Gib was not to go out of his way, he had to cross the old miser's fields.

Orasmus Petit was a grouchy old widower who hated all boys, and boys of Gib's age in particular. During the beginning of the school year, he always spent the early mornings guarding his precious apple orchard and was not above setting his vicious-looking hound Nettie after adventurous apple thieves.

As Gib drew near to the farmhouse and was about to cross through the corn field, he heard voices and stopped to hide before he was seen. Near the field was old Petit's vegetable patch. Beside it was a wagon pulled by a yoke of oxen. Two men were tossing cabbages into the wagon. They were Farmer Petit and Aaron Coon.

It seemed to Gib that he could not escape Mr. Coon, although it was logical enough for the storekeeper to be there bartering with the farmer for his crop of cabbages. Old Petit's vegetables were highly prized in the village.

But if he were not to be seen by the two men, Gib would have to go around the field, considerably out of his way. He pondered, and decided the added trip was worth the safety.

When he got across the bridge and arrived at the old gate on the Perrely land, panting from running, he found no one there. He called Djulih's name several times, but there was no answer. He realized it was long-past the time he was supposed to meet her, but he had hoped she would still be there. Certainly he could not go looking for her, for he had to be back home before his father returned.

Deeply disappointed, he started back. The whole desperate venture had been a failure.

Again he approached the Petit house and paused beside the corn field. He listened. There was no sound of voices. A bobwhite was calling nearby and was being answered by another a distance away. The yet unripe corn stirred in the wind like a restless green sea. He could see the vegetable patch quite clearly. The two men and the ox cart were gone. He moved in between two rows of corn.

Before he had quite reached the other side of the field, he became aware of the insistent baying of Petit's hound. Gib was sure the hound had seen him. He scrambled out of the corn field, prepared to run for his life. But once out of the field, he stopped. That was no ordinary sound Nettie was making. There was a note of fear in it. It was so insistent that Gib forgot his own sense of urgency and turned toward the farmhouse.

He climbed over a wooden rail fence and started running. Something very strange was going on. He could hear irregular hammering coming from the barn back of the house. And the cattle in there were bellowing crazedly. Still Gib moved cautiously around the house, until he saw smoke belching out of the barn door.

The barn was on fire! Now Gib understood. The oxen were tied up in their stall inside and were kicking frantically to escape. At that moment, Gib saw Nettie. He picked up a stick, prepared to defend himself. The hound ran toward him; but she made no effort to attack him, only uttered a series of short sharp barks. Somehow she had hurt her leg and was limping badly. She went back toward the barn, and seemed to be trying to show Gib where the fire was.

Gib moved nearer to the barn door and paused. He wondered what to do. There was no sign of Mr. Petit. He must have driven off with Mr. Coon. There was a bucket with some water in it beside the well. He picked it up and hurried into the barn, but backed out of the door at once, coughing furiously. There was so much smoke inside he could not see. One bucket of water was useless.

Nevertheless, he had to go back in to rescue the cattle. He ripped off his shirt and hastily tied it around his face to cover his nose and mouth. Then he went cautiously in.

There was a burst of flame from one side of the barn, which showed Gib where the oxen were tethered. There were three of them, plunging and kicking in their confined spaces like bucking horses. He could not approach them from behind and had to scramble over the side of the first stall to untie the rope that held the first beast's head in a noose. With the release of the rope, the ox reared backwards out of the stall and plunged, still kicking and bellowing, out through the door.

Gib succeeded in releasing all three of the oxen, but had his shirt torn from his face by the long spreading horn of the last ox as it twisted its head in a wild effort to escape.

Coughing, his eyes stinging and almost blinded, Gib stumbled toward the door. He could see that by now one side of the barn was a steady blaze and that a fence connecting the house and the barn was already burning like a fuse, the flames traveling with the help of the wind toward the house.

Struck by the danger threatening the house, Gib shouted wildly for Mr. Petit. He even rushed to the back door of the house and pounded on it, as if he expected the farmer to be inside. The hound howled piteously, like a stray wolf, with one paw raised.

Gib stopped his pounding and began looking for the bucket. Perhaps he could raise water from the well in time to throw it on the fence. But his frantic search was useless, for he soon realized he must have left the bucket in the barn. His eyes fell upon an ax leaning against the wall of the house.

He was well used to axes and lifted it high to bring it down on the top rail of the fence. If he could chop the

fence down in time, he could save the house. Again and again he swung, but the wood was locust and weathered with age. By the time the top rail splintered and broke, the flames from the barn were moving fast along the second rail. Gib was out of breath now and wondered where the strength would come from to smash the rest of the fence.

At this moment a voice spoke from behind, a controlled authoritative voice, "Give me the ax, Gib Martindale."

Gib turned. It was Philander. He handed over the ax with a sob of relief.

"Ye hold my rifle," said Philander.

Gib took it, holding the barrel.

In Philander's hands the ax whistled through the air in repeated strokes, severing the remaining fence rails almost one at a stroke. Then with one final blow of the ax head, Philander struck the nearest post to the ground.

"That's done it," Philander said, sending the ax in a neat curve in the air till the blade buried itself deep in a log some yards away. He took back his gun.

"Well, reckon Orasmus Petit's got a heap to thank ye fur, Gib. Saw how ye saved the oxen outer the barn."

"Did you?" said Gib foolishly.

"Clumbed a tree up yonder an' saw it. But I came too late to help ye." Then Philander added shortly, "Don't tell anyone I came." And he strode off out of sight.

The flames were steadily eating up the barn by now.

Gib turned and ran toward the village.

It was Mr. Tibbals, the blacksmith, who met him first. "Why Gib Martindale, what's thee been up to . . ."

Gib poured out the news—the Petit barn in flames.

Tibbals let out a roar, and his two sons, as large as himself, came out of the shop. With buckets in their hands, all three rushed off down the road, leaving Gib standing dazed. His attempt to get down to the valley unseen was shattered. His father would get to know now that he had climbed out of his bedroom window.

As he stood there, uncertain, the bell of the meeting house began to toll wildly. Someone had seen the flames and smoke at the Petit farm. The whole village would come running to the spot.

Gib moved off the road. He was in no condition to be seen. His body was smudged with dirt and smoke. His shirt was hardly more than a rag, ready to be thrown into the pile that would eventually be bartered to the peddler or at the general store. Even his pantaloons had a large rip in the right knee.

Forlornly, he started back through the woods toward home.

Before he reached home, he had at least thought out his plan of action. There was always the chance that the excitement of the fire might cause Mr. Tibbals to forget to speak of Gib's appearance on the road. He would just have to operate on this hope. Then if he could manage to get back to his room unseen, he could wash himself at the washstand in his room. His pantaloons he could mend or perhaps hide until the storm had blown over.

A fire in the neighborhood of Sturbridge was not a common thing. The excitement would bring every able-bodied person to the scene. He heard the rumble and shouting in the distance as the volunteer firemen began their dash down the road, pulling the little fire tub behind them. Gib wished he could stay to see it working. The machine could throw water on the flames in a steady stream as the men kept pumping and as long as the buckets could keep it filled with water. If there were enough buckets and enough water, the fire could at least be controlled.

As Gib expected, he found the house deserted and was easily able to sneak in through the back door. He climbed the stairs to his room. But he had forgotten that he had locked his room from the inside.

There was no alternative. He must go back down and try to climb up to the window from the outside.

Gib Accused

THE bell of the meeting house was still wrecking the air with its clamor, and he could hear the breathless voices of people as they ran across the green to get to the scene of the blaze.

The parlor window directly below his bedroom window was completely flush with the red clapboard sides. There was nowhere to place his feet. He would have to get the ladder from the barn. It was lucky Lovina was not in the kitchen to see him hauling the ladder out.

He leaned it up against the house where it reached his window easily. He scrambled up and was about to place his foot across to the window ledge when a high screech came from below, "Gib Martindale, what in the name of the good Lord are ye doin' up there!"

It was Granny Hope!

It was so obviously impossible for him to explain the whole thing that he shouted back like an idiot, "Nothing!"

"Oh, nothing is it?" Granny Hope was waving her walking stick up at him, and Gib's quick glance gave him the impression that she was dancing like a scalp-hungry Indian. "*Nothing* is it?" she was crying again. "*Nothing* that makes you run around half-naked! *Nothing* makes you as grimy as a chimbley sweep! Oh yes, your father will think *nothing* when he hears of this!" And of course that meant that Granny Hope would see that he did. "Come down at once, young savage, or *nothing* will end up worse than it is."

But all this screeching into the air was half lost on Gib, whose one desire was to get out of sight through the window. He did, though not without some dangerous slipping, which made Granny Hope more abusive than ever. Gib closed the window and collapsed on the floor exhausted.

Now all his plans had gone awry. Mr. Tibbals the blacksmith and his two sons might forget to talk of Gib, but there was little mercy in Granny Hope. He could not remember when she had been other than bitter and vengeful. She seemed never to have a good word for anybody.

Gib wondered if she would come screeching up the stairs to blast at the door with her stick. But there was a severe silence. Instead, she must be stirring her pot of trouble in the kitchen, he thought.

He got himself off the floor finally and washed and dressed in clean clothes. The ladder was still outside against the wall. But he couldn't go down the stairs again. And what was the use now, with Granny Hope after his scalp.

He sat at his window and did his best to patch up the rip in the old pantaloons. Like most boys in the village, he had long ago learned how to sew; but he had to admit he did not do a very good job.

From time to time he looked across the valley. At first he could see the smoke from the fire being carried by the wind, but after about an hour it dwindled to nothing. Gib concluded that the buckets and the fire tub had done their work, unless the barn had burned to ashes.

It was beginning to grow dark when he heard his father's chaise being driven into the barn. At the same time the front door was opened, and Gib could hear his mother talking to Lovina in loud tones. Then her footsteps came running up the stairs. Gib went to the door and opened it just as she arrived breathless, her face pale as a sheet.

"Gib, what have you done? Is it true that you were down at Orasmus Petit's farm when the fire broke out? I told your father it could not be."

"Yes, Mother, I was," said Gib.

"Oh Gib, Gib!" was all Mrs. Martindale could say.

At that moment the front door opened. Men's voices talked excitedly in the hall. Then Gib's father shouted up the stair.

"Gibeon, are you there? Come down at once."

"Yes, father," Gib said, and he looked down at his bare feet and wished he had put on his shoes. His mother suddenly put her arms around him and kissed him on the cheek.

"Gib, I'm sorry!" She said no more, and Gib started down the stairs.

His father was waiting for him below, looking as stern as Gib had ever seen him. "I have a few questions to ask you," he said. "Mr. Coon and Mr. Petit are in the parlor. Go in there."

"Yes, sir," said Gib. He could do nothing but expect the worst from two such men, he supposed.

Sylvester Martindale walked into the room behind Gib. The room smelt musty. It was used on special occasions only. Aaron Coon and Orasmus Petit were standing together by the window so that Gib could barely see their faces. They said nothing.

"Sit down, gentlemen," said his father, and he called back into the hall, "Lovina, bring the lamp in here, will you."

No one spoke until Lovina had set the lamp on the table. Mr. Martindale sat down at his desk. He addressed Lovina as she was going out, "Close the door,

Lovina. There must be no interruptions."

As the door closed, Gib found himself the only one standing. He was facing the other three and felt like a prisoner being judged, or perhaps condemned.

"Gibeon," his father began, "I have brought you up to be honest, if nothing else. And I expect that you will speak the truth in this whole matter."

"Yes, sir," said Gib.

"Were you down at Mr. Petit's place this afternoon?"

Gib had no chance to answer, for Farmer Petit shouted violently, "Of course he was. Didn't Aaron see him?"

"Let him answer for himself, sir," said his father. "Well, Gibeon?"

"Yes, sir," said Gib. "I was."

"There!" Farmer Petit thrust out a horny finger in triumph. "There!" And he jumped to his feet. He was a wizened wiry little man, quicker than a chipmunk, with a dry bitter tongue.

"There what?" said Gib's father. "That does not make him guilty, sir."

Gib was confused. What did they mean by being guilty? Guilty of what?

Orasmus Petit's high cracked voice rushed on, "Who else could it be but him? There warn't no one else there."

"Was there, Gibeon?" asked his father.

Gib hesitated. Philander had specifically asked him not to mention that he was there. He couldn't betray that trust, even if it meant a lie.

"Well, boy?" said his father impatiently. "Did you see anyone while you were there?"

Gib lowered his eyes. "No, sir." At least, he thought, there was no one there at the beginning.

"There, there! I told you," began Orasmus Petit again.

But Aaron Coon said gruffly, "At least he ain't tryin' to accuse someone else."

This made Gib wonder if Mr. Coon had seen Philander there as well. But surely if he had, he would say so.

Gib's father turned on the storekeeper angrily. "A Martindale does not tell a lie, Aaron."

Gib gulped. It was almost as if his father wanted to be on his son's side.

"Ask him what he was doin' there," insisted Farmer Petit. "See what he says to that."

"Well," said Sylvester, "you sit down then, Orasmus, and give the boy a chance." He turned to Gib. "I think you'd better tell your story in your own way, Gibeon." There was even a note of sympathy in his voice.

Gib described how he had jumped out of the window when no one was around except Lovina, who was too busy cleaning the sitting room to see him. Then he had gone through the woods.

"Ask him what time it was?" snapped Farmer Petit, as if it was of great concern.

"I don't know," Gib explained. "I didn't see a clock."

"Of course he wouldn't say," muttered Aaron Coon.

"But I didn't see any clock," Gib insisted, but his father cut him off.

"Go on with your story, son."

Gib told how he was walking through the farmer's corn field when he heard the dog's frightened howling.

"But what was he doin' there on the farm in the first place?" asked Aaron Coon.

"I was . . . I was just walking there . . ."

"Trespassing?" asked Aaron Coon pointedly, while Orasmus Petit stared at Gib with sparkling beady eyes.

Gib found it hard to explain that he was on his way back from the valley. He hoped they wouldn't ask.

"Ye were in my barn, boy. Why don't ye say so?" shouted Mr. Petit, jumping to his feet and bouncing down again.

"I did go in," said Gib, glad not to have to speak of the valley.

"Why?"

"Because of the fire. I tried to put it out."

"You'd set it alight. So now ye took fright an' tried to put it out."

That was from Orasmus Petit. Gib stared at him in astonishment. Was the man really accusing him, Gib, of starting the fire? Since no one else objected to the suggestion, not even his father, Gib cried out, "But I didn't start the fire. You don't really think that?"

"You said there warn't nobody else there," observed Aaron Coon drily.

"But I didn't want to set fire to Mr. Petit's barn," Gib shouted, beginning to forget his reserve.

"Ain't sayin' ye did want to," explained Aaron Coon.

"Young sinners! Allus up to deviltry!" Orasmus Petit was shouting.

"I didn't," Gib shouted just as loudly. "I came there because Nettie was bawling. The barn was already on fire when I got there."

"It's a lie! It's a lie!" Farmer Petit jumped wildly to his feet and was going into a strange little dance of hysterics.

"Sit down," said Sylvester Martindale, so sternly that Orasmus sat down abruptly. "Now, Gibeon, how long had the fire been burning when you got there?"

"Well, the barn was filled with smoke, and flames were coming out of the side," explained Gib.

"Then perhaps half an hour?" asked his father.

"Yes, sir."

"Now, you walked through the woods from this house to get to Mr. Petit's place?"

"Yes, sir."

"That should take about half an hour's walking."

Gib guessed so, and wondered what his father was leading to.

"That means you left this house by the window at about four o'clock, for that was when the fire started in the barn."

"Four o'clock, sir? I don't know. I didn't see a clock."

"But it must have been about four," insisted his father, "for you to reach the barn half an hour after the fire started? Isn't that so?"

Gib looked into his father's eyes, worried. "I suppose so, sir."

"Don't you see, Gibeon, if I can establish when you left this house by the window I can prove that you could not have been at the barn early enough to start the fire, as Mr. Petit thinks you did. Right?"

"Oh," said Gib. "Yes, sir. I do see. But I didn't have a clock to look at."

"Yes, yes, I know," his father cut him off. "But you climbed out of the window when Lovina was cleaning the front room. So you said just now."

"Yes, sir."

Sylvester Martindale rose from his chair and went to the door. All eyes were on him. Even Orasmus Petit sat still waiting expectantly. Gib felt his pulse pounding with a strange premonition of danger.

Lovina came shuffling into the room with a scowl of suspicion on her face.

"Lovina, you cleaned the sitting room this afternoon, didn't you?"

"Reckon there ain't nothing wrong with that," muttered Lovina, lifting her head resentfully.

"No, Lovina," said the doctor. "Of course not. But I want you to tell me what time it was."

"It was jest afore I went to the back to pick them beans."

"You went straight into the garden after you had finished the dining room, is that it?"

"Yes, sir, I did. An' who's goin' to tell me different?"

"Do you know what time it was when you left the sitting room?"

"Yes, sir, it was not more'n two o'clock."

"Two o'clock!" exclaimed Mr. Martindale, glancing at Gib.

"I said two o'clock, 'cos it were two o'clock."

There was a moment's silence, then Gib's father asked, "You didn't come back to the sitting room later, say around four?"

"No, sir. I never come back to that room. I'd finished it proper."

Sylvester nodded abruptly, and Lovina moved herself out of the room.

Orasmus Petit was now out of his chair again. "There, there, there!"

Gib felt he had been caught with the most horrible lie. His father said, as if talking to himself, "So it was two, not four, when Gibeon climbed out of the window."

"I tol' you I seed him snoopin' around the farm afore we left," said Aaron Coon.

"Then what was he doin' from two to four?" shrieked Orasmus, waving his hand in the air and dancing violently about. "In my barn, that's what he was doin'. In my barn sparkin' tinder, lightin' wicks. That's what he was doin'. Breakin' locks. Stealin', stealin'. The law 'tis'll settle this. I'm going to the constable. I'll have him in the stocks. I'll go to the county sheriff . . ."

"Orasmus," began Gib's father; but it wasn't any use. The wiry old farmer was so hopping mad, he was like one who had lost his wits; and when he rushed wildly for the door, no one tried to stop him.

Gib did not know what to say. To explain that he had not gone straight to the Petit place but that he had gone down to the valley and back he knew would no longer be believed. He felt hurt and resentful. It seemed to him he had been driven into a terrible corner and condemned before he had had a chance to tell the whole story. He could see that his father was hurt, too. When Aaron Coon tried to say something sympathetic, with the air of a friend at a funeral, Sylvester cut him off and asked him to leave.

When the front door closed, the doctor turned to his son, "Gibeon, did you start that fire in the barn? Answer me straight, yes or no."

"No, sir," said Gib emphatically.

His father looked at him a moment, as if his eyes were trying to bury deep into the boy's mind. Then he said quietly, "But how can I believe you?"

He turned on his heel and walked out of the house.

The Escape

BEING left like that without knowing what he should do was worse than being sent to his room. His mother came running into the room at once.

"Was that your father? Where did he go?"

"I don't know," said Gib dejectedly.

When she saw the expression on his face, she rushed forward. "Gib, what has happened?"

She smothered him in her arms, so that Gib had difficulty making himself heard.

"They say that I set fire to that crabby old Petit's barn."

His mother said, "Hush, Gib, hush!" And she rocked

him a little. "And you told them you didn't."

"They say I lie."

"But your father?"

"He doesn't believe me either."

Lydia ceased her rocking for a moment of shocked stillness. Then she held Gib away from her and stared at him as if she couldn't believe her ears. Finally, she spoke in a strained, breathless voice. "Go up and put your shoes on. We'll go to Mr. Bownum. He must speak to your father."

The village outside was in disorder. The Petit fire had introduced a sense of general uneasiness. The people were reacting like ruffled chickens, as if protection could only be sought in each other's company. They had gathered in groups to talk about it, and the day's business seemed at a standstill.

The darkness of early evening had come down, and so many people held lanterns in their hands that the scene looked like a festival. All that was lacking was the sound of fireworks.

Gib's mother, unlike the others, had purpose. She swept up the road like a little ship in full sail toward the parish house at the end of the green. It was hard for Gib, for he found himself too often falling behind her as she threaded in and out of the clusters of people. He had to run repeatedly to keep abreast of her. She said nothing to anyone. Those who greeted her got no reply. Gib sensed that conversations stopped abruptly as they approached, and he felt eyes spearing into his back as they passed.

Gib did not know how much the people knew of his part in the whole affair. He could not help thinking that they must know everything, and, like Orasmus Petit and Aaron Coon and even his father, were condemning him for a terrible wickedness. He expected no kindness from the Reverend Mr. Bownum either.

A voice called out to Gib, almost in his ear, "Well, Gib, heard you set fire to old crabby Petit's barn." It was followed by the familiar laugh of Willis Pickle. "Wish I'd thought of that."

There was a chorus of appreciative laughter from Willis' band of friends. For not the first time, Gib wished that Timothy were home. He'd take care of that Willis Pickle. But Gib said nothing. He kept his eyes to the ground. His mother, however, turned on them in a fury. "Go home," she shouted, as if she were talking to a herd of sniffing beasts. "And go home, you, Willis Pickle, and you mind your own affairs."

The boys chortled from a safe distance and ran off.

The Bownums, like most of the village people, had been to the fire and were just settling down into their house again. Elijah Bownum looked very grave indeed. Yes, he had heard of the talk against Gib. He did not say he didn't believe it, but talked of compassion and forgiveness. Indeed he delivered a little sermon of complaint against the people, although never once speaking of Gib's innocence.

Gib still said nothing. He felt choked up and doubted

that words could come out of him if asked to speak. His mother began to weep, all her purpose melting away, until her condition became the important thing to be dealt with. The situation became so bad that the parson went to the door and called his wife; and Mrs. Bownum, acting as if hysterical mothers were an everyday affair, took Gib by the arm and led him out of the room without a word and closed the door.

"You come into the kitchen," she said, "and never mind, never mind at all. Your mother's something upset, poor dear."

Gib was pressed into a chair and given a stick of striped barley candy to suck, as if he were an infant to be kept amused.

Mrs. Bownum paid no more attention to him then, as she concentrated on her needlework. Restless, Gib looked out of the window and saw that the moon, like the night before, was lighting up the scene in rich silver.

Gib liked the moon. He liked the whole night outside among the trees and the fields and the wild creatures. He liked the night better than what went on in the house, full of suspicions and fears and uncertainties.

A sudden desire to be out there possessed him. Without thinking, he got up off his chair and walked to the back door.

"Gib!" He heard Mrs. Bownum's puzzled call. "Gib." But he paid no attention. He opened the door and ran out. Mrs. Bownum called agitatedly. She brought her lamp to the doorway and peered out after him; but Gib

had started to run, and he did not stop. He did not know where he was going and did not care, so long as he felt he was moving away from the village.

He supposed it was panic that had seized him, for he ran as if he were being chased, but he felt at the same time a kind of power and a kind of joy. He stumbled over many obstacles on the ground, for the moon's light was not strong enough to show him everything; and springy branches came up and struck him across the body and face, but it didn't matter. He kept his steady pace through the meadows, and he only stopped when he felt his shoes sticking to wet mud.

He stood panting. The night was warm and pleasant. The light was growing stronger as the moon rose high. He felt much better. It was as if the light of the moon had entered inside him and renewed his belief in himself.

He looked about but could not decide where he was. He could hear the sound of a creek splashing over pebbles. He climbed to a hummock of grass and removed his shoes. It was easier to walk without them. He tied the laces together and hung them around his neck.

He could see the gleaming of the creek a few yards away and moved down into it. The water felt cool through his toes. Without considering his direction, he followed the flow of the water. He did not let himself think solidly about anything. All he sensed was that he was moving deliciously away from trouble and becoming freer every step he took.

After some time he saw a plank bridge that crossed the creek. He climbed out of the water and moved up the steep bank to the road above. He did not recognize anything, and so he set off in a direction he imagined would lead away from all his accusers in the village.

He followed the road steadily, up and down the hills, thrilling at the sound of animal movements in the hedges, his eyes tracing the silver tops of trees and by their outlines establishing their kind.

It seemed to Gib that he had been walking for hours before he sensed that he was getting sleepy. When he came to a field then, where heaps of hay lay still un-gathered, he turned in through the gate and lay down in the soft warmth to rest.

The next thing he knew the sun was flashing in his eyes. He had slept the night completely away; dawn had come and passed, for the sun was up above the trees. He got to his feet, a sense of excitement filling his whole body. He half expected to have to run for his life from hordes of pursuers, like an escaped slave running away from a southern plantation. He had heard about these poor Negroes, though he had never seen them. It was to Canada they went if they were success-ful in eluding their pursuers. Perhaps he would go to Canada, too. He judged from the sun which direction was north and started walking.

The road was full of cart ruts that had hardened in the cool of the night. They made walking rather diffi-cult. After going several miles, he suddenly realized he had forgotten his shoes. He stopped. Should he go back? But what use were shoes, anyway, other than for going to the meeting house on the Sabbath? He went on.

His stomach began to feel empty. He hoped he would pass an orchard and find some fruit. How did escaping slaves, traveling all those hundreds of miles from the South, find food to keep themselves alive? They did have people who helped them on their way, Gib remembered, people who gave them food and shelter during the day so that they could run all through the night. Would anyone help a runaway white boy who didn't know where he was going and wouldn't say why he had left home or where his home was?

When he came to a farmhouse or a village, he decided, he would have to try to find work in exchange for food or he would really starve.

He walked on and on, but there was no sign of a house of any kind. He began to feel thoroughly miserable, and a fear took hold of him. His feet began to falter. He tried to keep his mind off home, but he couldn't. He kept wondering what his father and mother were doing. Were they looking for him? Or were they just waiting for him to return on his own? Well, he wouldn't. He wouldn't live with people who had no faith in his honesty.

At that moment his foot hit a heavy stone, and he found himself sprawled on the ground. He had not hurt himself, but he didn't get up at once. He felt his cheek and realized he was crying. Crying without knowing it! That was strange.

His ears caught a sound in the air. At first he thought it was a dog barking in the distance. Perhaps it indicated the presence of some farm. But then he decided it was more musical. It was a man's voice. As he listened, he could hear the wheels of a cart and the measured beat of hoofs on the road beyond the bend ahead. A horse and cart were approaching. The sound was that of a man singing.

Gib sat up. What should he do? This was the first person he had encountered since his escape from Sturbridge. Should he hide himself away? He got up and concealed himself behind a hedge, to wait and see.

The cart came slowly round the bend, for the horse was walking quite leisurely. Gib could see that it was an ordinary four-wheeled farm wagon, painted a dirty red. It had a looped canvas cover over it, like a smaller edition of those wagons that people lived in when they went off into the western territory to make their homes. The driver held the reins quite slack and leaned back letting his horse choose her own lazy pace. His face was lifted to the clouds, and he was letting his voice roar forth in a joyous song.

The whole picture was one of a man perfectly contented with himself. He was a smallish man with a rather large head and a great bush of unruly hair that reached down his neck. Gib watched amazed and began to feel happy just watching. He almost ran out and asked for a lift. He realized just in time that the cart was going in the wrong direction.

And then, with a sudden start, Gib knew who it was. This was the peddler, Pardon Perrely! This was the father of Philander; the father of Djulih!

In the middle of a phrase, in the middle of a word, the man stopped singing; and the next words soared out as if really part of the song: "Woa, Lovely!" The horse came to a quiet, unhurried stop.

Gib stared. Why was he stopping? The peddler didn't get down from his cart. He sat back comfortably and let his eyes slowly scan the landscape. When he spoke, it was quietly into the hot sunny silence. "Ah, the mornin' is lovely this mornin'. Ain't it lovely, Lovely?" Gib decided the mare's name must be Lovely, and to his surprise the beast shook her head up and down several times. "And I'm calculatin' ye'd just love to go scamperin' out in them medders like as if ye was nothin' but a lanky-shanked, knock-kneed filly all over agin, ain't that there the truth of it, Lovely?"

The mare actually nodded again and let out a delicious snort through her nostrils. The peddler laughed. "I knowed it; I knowed it; but there's some things I don't know, come to think on it. For instance now, Lovely, kin ye explain to me why young fellers hide theirselves behind bushes as though hit warn't good to be seen on such a glory day? 'Cos I'm thinkin' there ain't nothin' in this whole stretch o' world that'd fail to be in its prime best under such a mornin'."

Gib couldn't believe his ears. Was the peddler speaking of him?

"How long are we goin' to have to wait, Lovely, afore this young feller comes out and says a good mornin' to us'n?"

Feeling very sheepish, Gib walked out from behind the bush and onto the road.

"Well now, Lovely," said the peddler to the mare, hardly giving Gib more than a glance, "that was worth waitin' fur, warn't it?" Then he turned to Gib, and his pink-cheeked rugged face creased up into a broad smile and his blue eyes fairly danced as he patted the seat beside him. "Come up alongside o' me, young-un, where ye kin see better, an' the three of us'll do some praisin' o' the weather."

Gib felt the honest warmth of the man and readily climbed up beside him.

"Now see them fields with the sun slantin' on 'em."

Gib nodded. "Yes, sir."

"That's the way God paints 'em. An' don't let anyone try to tell ye different, for no man kin do it like He do it. Ye see, all we got t'do is to try to copy Him, an' if'n we kin get real close to it, we're smilin'; then we're really smilin'."

"But how does one copy it?" asked Gib.

"Well now, there's ways. Fer instance like, ye kin pick up all the colors o' the rainbow, each at a time, with a artist's brush smaller than the tip o' yer little finger, an' set 'em down careful-like on a stretch o' canvas, an' mebbe light'll come into ye, an' ye'll do it close. But there's other ways o' copyin' God. Ye've jest got to find yer own way."

"Yes, sir. I suppose so, sir."

"Well," said Pardon Perrely, slapping Gib on the knee, "ye suppose so now, but mebbe ye'll get to know so later."

He jiggled the reins and clucked his tongue at the mare, and Lovely began a jaunty walk. "Smells her own barn by now. Lovely's gettin' spiritful."

Gib leaned against the seat, letting the jerking of the cart possess his body. He felt a glow of restfulness. For the moment it didn't worry him that he was going back the way he had come. Pardon Perrely was silent for a while, too. This was Philander's father, and Djulih's father. Gib tried to feel the resemblance. He seemed much more like Djulih than Philander. Philander, Gib supposed, took after his mother in his solemn ways and few words, while Djulih could be gay and talkative like her father. Suddenly, he heard the peddler saying, "What brings ye so far from home? Is it business ye kin talk upon?"

Gib laughed, "Am I far away from home?"

"If ye're Doc Martindale's boy, as I fancy ye are, then ye won't be back home till near evenin' at the rate Lovely likes best."

"I don't want to go back," Gib blurted out, although he made no effort to get off the cart.

"Sometimes, when somethin's wrong," said the peddler looking off into the fields, "it's best to stay out o' the way; then agin it could be better still to face it out."

"How can you face it out," asked Gib earnestly, "when no one'll believe what you say?"

"Makes it kind o' hard," agreed Pardon Perrely. "It do seem strange how folks prefer to hunt up evil than to find good."

For Gib, this was the first time he felt like talking to anyone about his troubles. The fact that the peddler didn't ask him any more questions helped a great deal. And soon Gib found himself relating the incidents concerning the Petit fire. But he did not speak of Philander or of Djulih. He did not know how Pardon Perrely would like a Martindale trespassing on Perrely land. He wondered if the peddler knew or cared anything about the ancient feud. It didn't seem likely that he didn't know something about it, and he might prefer to keep off the subject.

"Well," said Pardon Perrely, after Gib had finished, "there is no way of puttin' a man in jail without proof o' his bein' guilty. Orasmus Petit'll find it easier to shout it out that ye're guilty than to prove ye are."

"But they'll all go on thinking I'm guilty," said Gib miserably.

"Well, there's two kin play that game, boy. You go on statin' ye're innocent until everybody's tired of the arguin', and they'll begin to believe ye."

"But what about my father?" asked Gib.

"He'll believe ye, too. Fer the Martindale's don't like

anyone callin' 'em liars."

"Is it wrong to be that way?" asked Gib.

"A man kin be any way he wants, jest as long as it don't hurt nobody else, I calculate."

"But that's just what the Martindales have done."

The peddler glanced at him. "Have they now?"

That was the nearest Gib got to speaking of the family feud. He had the feeling that Pardon Perrely would prefer not to speak of it, for he abruptly changed the conversation.

"Are ye feared o' gettin' switched when ye get home? That ain't what's keepin' ye from home, is it?"

"No," said Gib. "I don't care about that."

"Good," said the peddler. "When ye be gettin' a switchin', allus think o' somethin' else. There ain't no switch in the world big enough to make a man wrong when he's right."

Gib looked at the peddler happily. "Do you think I've told the truth, Mr. Perrely?"

"There ain't no Martindale in the world kin tell a lie," was the prompt answer; and Pardon Perrely winked and went into a loud sonorous laugh.

Gib was happy. He knew that at last he had a friend among the grownups.

The peddler handed him a basket of blackberries to eat while he began to talk of his travels. Gib learned that he had done what he called a "thrivin' business" in painting portraits. "Folks like to have theirselves and sometimes their houses set down all lifelike in colors.

Makes 'em feel kind o' high an' mighty-like," he said and laughed. "So I'm back afore the snows o' winter sets in. I'll paint my cart with a new coat of the reddest paint I kin mix up, an' patch her up an' grease her up. An' Lovely there kin gambol about the medders to her blessed ol' heart's content."

The cart had come over the brow of a small hill. Sturbridge was not far in the distance, for the spire of the meeting house was already visible above the trees. A group of horsemen were riding swiftly toward them. As soon as they were in earshot, they began shouting: "Gib, Gib! Is that Gib Martindale?"

The man in the lead was young Silas Bushaw, who was Aaron Coon's assistant at the general store. He was followed by the two massive sons of Tibbals the black-smith and the elegant young Jesse Gaylord, the taver-ner's son. They surrounded the cart like sheriff's men so that Pardon Perrely had to pull Lovely up short.

"Hey, peddler," shouted Silas Bushaw, "what ye doin' running' off with the boy? His father's lookin' for him."

The peddler looked at him scornfully. "If I be run-nin' off with the boy, then, by jimminy, I reckon my hoss is a-walkin' backwards."

Jesse Gaylord let out a high whinny of laughter, and the Tibbals boys grinned. But Silas scowled as he turned to Gib. "Ye'd better get yourself back home sharp, Gib Martindale. The whole village, includin' the constable, is out scourin' the woods for ye."

"I'm coming home," said Gib.

Jesse Gaylord eased his horse to the side of the cart. "Here, get up behind me, Gib," he said. "We'll get you back faster than the peddler can."

Gib hesitated. He looked at Pardon Perrely, who nodded encouragement.

"Hold me tight," shouted Jesse, as he put spurs to his horse.

Gib turned in time to shout back to the peddler, "Thank you, Mr. Perrely."

The man shouted back, "Remember, Gib." And he slapped the cart again and again with his whip. "Think o' somethin' else when it happens."

A "Trial" in the Meetinghouse

News of Gib's return seemed to have reached the village almost before the horsemen came galloping up to the Martindale house. People shot out of their doors, so that Gib had to get down off Jesse's horse into the midst of a crowd.

Everybody wanted to ask him questions and to get his attention. They pulled at his arms until he was tossed about like a leaf in a wind. Not until his father came out of the front door, shouting, did everyone fall back to make way for him.

His father clutched at Gib's arm and shook him a little. "Gib, where have you been?" There was relief in his voice more than anger. He pushed him toward the door, where his mother came runing to smother him with tearful affection.

Gib had said nothing all the while. He seemed to be living in a kind of dream. Nothing touched him. He heard his father talking to the neighbors, thanking them for their concern, and he felt his mother's caresses and her tears, all as if he were not really present.

His mother pulled him into the house, and his father came in closing the door.

"Gibeon," said his father.

"Yes, sir." Then he added, "I'm sorry, sir. I should never have run away."

"So you did run away! Why? Is it because you did it—set fire to his barn? Because that's certainly the way you've made it look."

"No, sir. It was because you didn't believe me when I told you I didn't. But I don't care now."

'Don't care?"

"You will punish me, sir, I know, because I climbed out of the window. But you can't punish me for doing something I never did. And my truth won't turn into a lie no matter how hard you beat me."

Gib felt his mother's quick intake of breath, as if she was afraid of what his father might do. Gib looked up at his father fearfully even as he said it. It was the way the peddler had put it. At first Sylvester Martindale stared, disbelieving. Then his frown suddenly vanished, and he looked at his wife and laughed.

"Mrs. Martindale, our son has turned into a man!" His eyes found Gib again, "No, son, I believe you now."

"Thank you, sir," said Gib.

"But, Gibeon," his father said, as he moved forward and laid his hands on Gib's shoulders, "it's not going to be easy for you, or me."

As if to reinforce his words, there came a sharp rap on the door. Sylvester glanced out of the sitting room window, then turned to his wife. "Lydia, take Gibeon into the kitchen and close the door. It's the constable."

Before Gib's mother could make a move, however, the front door was thrown open, and Orasmus Petit darted in followed by Asa Chubb, the huge and breathless constable. Behind them came a press of curious villagers, pushing and shoving to get into the entry way.

Sylvester Martindale faced them, furious, and shouted above the clamor, "What right have any of you to invade the privacy of my home?"

But Orasmus Petit was shrieking and pointing at Gib, "There he is, there! He can't escape now. I've got the constable with me."

The clamor of voices that followed was drowned out by the giant roar of Constable Chubb, "You listen, all of you, to me. I ain't here to jail anybody, and, Doctor Martindale, I want ye to know I don't hold with breakin' into any man's house to accuse 'em. But folks are allowin' theirselves to get mighty worked up about this whole thing, an' somethin' has to be done afore people start doin' things they'll be sorry fur later."

"If you mean you want to question my son," said Gib's father, "you can't do it like this. First, he's got to get some rest and some food in him. Second, justice isn't going to be served in the heat of emotions."

"When then, when?" shouted Orasmus. "Don't let him get out of it."

"Tomorrow," said Sylvester Martindale, "at two hours before noon at the meetinghouse. I will be there with my son, and providing the meeting can be held in the customarily orderly way. Anyone who wishes can ask what questions he wants. There this matter can be settled once and for all."

"That's fair 'nough," roared Asa Chubb, before anyone else could speak; and he pressed back against the crowd, which yielded and opened the way for him and the muttering Orasmus Petit to pass through.

Once more Sylvester Martindale closed the door, and the crowd slowly dispersed.

The meetinghouse next morning was a sight to see. Gib wouldn't have imagined that so many people could be packed into the building. There was an air of great excitement. Everyone acted as if they had come to be entertained. It was hard for Gib to realize that this was the meetinghouse where the parson preached his sermons each sober Sabbath morning. For now the building was not big enough to contain the crowd who wanted to listen to old Orasmus Petit, the miser, screeching like a madman against Gib Martindale.

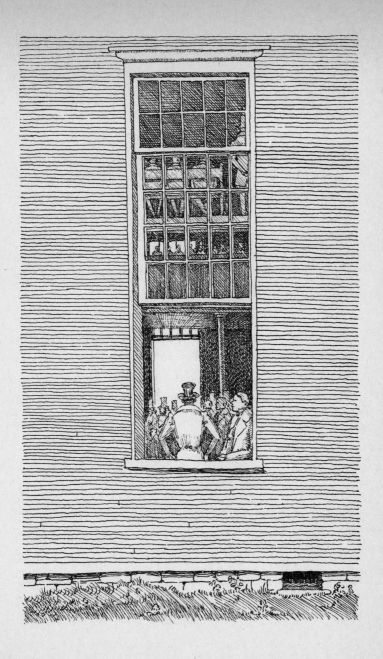

It had already been decided early that morning that no women and children would be allowed to enter. The meeting would be conducted as much as possible like a town meeting, but even the gallery was crammed with people. Some enterprising youths had gone as far as to climb up on the window ledges from the outside, and no one shouted them off. The pillared porch and the doors were jammed with people who couldn't get into the hall; and all the windows along the side of the meeting-house were wide open so that other folks who couldn't get in could stand outside and listen. Carts and wagons had been drawn up alongside the building so that folks could see in through the windows.

Gib had come to the meetinghouse with his father quite early. He sat on the platform between his father and the Reverend Mr. Bownum. A little to one side were Orasmus Petit and the constable. Between them were the officials of Sturbridge, besides Gib's father, the selectmen, Aaron Coon and Hannibal Sage.

Hannibal Sage, the shoemaker, had been chosen to open the proceedings, since he was the only one of the selectmen uninvolved in the Petit affair. He rose and stood before the gathering, looking very small, his hand running through his mass of unruly hair. Did he feel that just standing there would be sufficient to quiet them? Finally he threw up his hands and jerked his head, letting out a high pitched yell, which if it was a word or a sentence could not be detected as that. It rang though the meetinghouse and for a moment startled the people into silent attention.

"Silence," shouted Hannibal into the silence, and there was some laughter. But the shoemaker did not allow things to get out of his control again. He told them that this was a very solemn occasion, for when man accuses man, whether rightly or wrongly, it is time to be terribly just.

"Now if Matthew Larabee is here, as I see he is," he went on, turning to where the farmer was sitting quite near the platform, "let him start us up on a psalm. 'The Lord will come and he will not . . .' "

Farmer Larabee loved to sing and sprang to his feet instantly, not letting Hannibal finish the beginning words of the hymn, but letting his massive voice roll out, ". . . keep silence, but speak out."

At once the meetinghouse was rocked into a fervent religious gathering. All sang lustily, and when the strains of the hymn died away, Hannibal asked the parson to open the meeting with a prayer.

As Hannibal had suspected, the singing served to give a sense of union to the gathering, and the prayer quieted them into a proper sense of reverence, so that he was able to make his opening remarks without interruption.

He told his listeners that this was an unusual problem they had before them. It was not a business meeting, and it was not a court of law. "Now," he explained, "I've talked to Doctor Martindale, and it is his opinion that the community has a right to hear all sides of the

question. His son's not of age. Whatever he's done—
if he's done anythin'—that his father's willin' to pay for.
That's fair enough, ain't it? But it's got to be proved . . ."

"What proof's wantin' more?" shouted a voice.
"Didn't the barn burn down?" Gib could see it came
from Silas Bushaw, sitting in the gallery and being
urged on by a group of younger men of the village.

Some of the older folk agreed with Bushaw, but
others did not; and since everyone shouted at once, the
meeting nearly got out of hand again. Just the same, a
good handful of responsible men frowned on the disorder and stood up calling for quiet. In a moment of
silence, Hannibal was able to get in a warning: he
would call on the constable to throw the noisemakers
out of the building. This had the desired effect.

What he proposed to do, Hannibal Sage went on,
was to let the two sides have their say. First of all, the
evidence would be brought up against the accused, that
is Gib; then Gib would be allowed to defend himself
by telling his side of the story. Then there would be
some questioning, followed by a vote of all present by a
show of hands.

Since no one objected to this arrangement, Hannibal
called on Aaron Coon to tell as much as he knew of
that day of the barn burning. He described in somber
terms how he had been out in the cabbage patch with
Orasmus Petit when he caught a glimpse of Doctor
Martindale's son slipping round the field.

Gib's father sprang to his feet, "I object, Aaron. You

told me before you weren't certain it was my son."

Orasmus sprang to his feet, "He's talkin' out o' turn, Hannibal."

But Aaron nodded at Gib's father, "Sure, I reckon that's what I did say. But it did seem like it was your boy, right enough."

Next Moriah Tibbals was called on, and he stated that he had first heard of the fire when Gib came down the road about five o'clock, he guessed. He had run to the place then with his two sons, and they were the first to get to the fire.

"Why don't ye tell what the boy looked like on the road," shouted Orasmus Petit, who was finding it hard to remain in his seat so long.

Gib guessed Mr. Tibbals was being truthful enough when he said, "Well, Gib, I calculate that thee were a mite sooty."

Farmer Petit was called on then, and he fairly leaped from his seat to the platform. "Yes, yes, reckon I'll tell what I know. Me barn burned to the ground, leastways all but the one end. That's what I know. Ye all see'd it. And ye all know'd it was set alight by someone. No barn could have burned up of itself . . ."

"That ain't the truth, Orasmus, and you know that," interrupted farmer Larabee.

"Yes," shouted someone. "Go on Mr. Larabee. Prove it."

"Hay's been known to explode of its own accord when it's packed in a barn the wrong way . . ."

"Not mine," shouted Orasmus. "An' it'd been in there no more'n a week."

"Go on," shouted Silas Bushaw. "Go on, go on," came the cries all around him in the gallery.

"Go on I will," shrieked Orasmus. "There was two bits of evidence we found in that barn. First, there was a lantern up in the hayloft. A lantern taken up amongst that hay! That goes to prove somebody done it. An' I reckon it's not hard to guess who that somebody was." Orasmus glared across at Gib.

"We're not here for guessing," said Gib's father. "Stick to the facts."

"Well, I've proved the barn was set alight by somebody, ain't I?"

There was loud agreement from a sizable number in the hall, especially from up in the gallery.

"Then there was a box," Orasmus went on. "There was a box up in the loft. And that box was locked. Well, I found the lock. An' that there lock was opened."

He paused for effect, and then went on. "Don't that prove that somebody was up there tamperin' with that lock? The fire couldn't've unlocked it."

"Why not?" shouted someone from the back of the hall.

"If'n that's meant for a joke," shot back Orasmus, "it ain't a good one. The box was at the end of the barn that warn't burned."

Somebody wanted to know what was in the box.

"Money," snapped Orasmus.

"How much?"

"That ain't nobody's business. But whoever was up in the barn loft made it *his* business." He glared across at Gib again. "For all that was in the box was gone."

Gib was too filled with indignation to care about all the eyes staring at him curiously.

"Now, I'd like to talk about Doctor Martindale's boy. He was lyin' afore, when his pa questioned him. He said then he got to the barn when the fire'd already been burnin' fur a half hour. But his pa proved it his-self: the boy left his house a whole two hour afore that. Then what was he doin' fur two hours? Ask him that. And when he tells you his story, don't believe him none, fur it's goin' to be more lies."

Gib jumped to his feet. He could feel his face hot with emotion. "I didn't tell any lie. My father knows I didn't."

"Well, if ye didn't, ye let people think a thing was true when it weren't. That's as bad."

Sylvester Martindale said something that was lost in the sudden uproar of voices, and he pulled Gib back to his seat.

Hannibal called for order and told Farmer Petit to sit down a while and cool off, while Gib Martindale had a chance to tell his story.

Gib looked at his father, who leaned over and whispered, "Tell the truth, Gibeon. That's all that's necessary. Don't be afraid to tell the truth."

But it was not easy for Gib. He had to explain what

he was doing from the time he left the house to the time he arrived at the fire.

"I saw Mr. Coon and Mr. Petit collecting the cabbages. And then I went around the field."

He paused. What could he say? He could not draw Djulih into it.

"Well, what did you do then, Gib?" asked Hannibal helpfully.

"I went on down into the valley a bit."

"What fur?" shouted Orasmus Petit.

"Nothing," said Gib lamely.

"There, there," cried Petit. "He's lyin'."

"What's wrong with nothing?" said a voice from the pews. It was Gaylord the taverner. "It's my impression boys do 'nothing' most of their time, unless put to work by their parents."

There was much laughter at that, which made Gib feel relieved but a little foolish.

"Then what did you do, Gib?" asked Hannibal.

"Well, sir, I came back. Mr. Coon and Mr. Petit were gone, and I heard Mr. Petit's hound baying."

Petit was on his feet, "Are ye goin' to believe that? Two hours gone, jest wanderin' down the valley and back, fur nothin'. That's mighty convenient to say, ain't it? To come back jest in time to put the fire out. Reckon he thinks he's safe sayin' that, seein' there warn't nobody there to check on him."

"But it's the truth," cried Gib desperately.

"He han't explained yet," shouted Silas Bushaw,

"why he was snoopin' around the Petit farm in the first place."

Gib's father was on his feet.

"Why don't you let the boy tell his story?"

"Tall story," came a voice from the gallery, followed by loud laughter.

The meeting was getting out of hand again, for the two sides on the matter were shouting at each other. Hannibal Sage sprang to his feet, but at this point everyone was distracted by a sudden clamor from the entrance hall, loud voices, and the sound of some scuffling. Folks began turning around. Hannibal called out to know what was going on.

"Young feller here want to break in," someone shouted back. "Who does he think he is, the King of England?"

The rest was lost in the melee of protesting voices. Constable Chubb ran up the aisle to deal with the trouble. In a moment he was back, roaring across to Hannibal, "He's gone, I reckon. He was just . . ."

But he stopped with his mouth open, staring at the window to the right of him. In a sudden movement, the youths crowding the window ledge found themselves pressed to one side and a lithe figure sprang up, darkly outlined against the sky beyond. He stood there a moment. Everyone turned to the window, startled.

Someone shouted, "By jimminy, it's the peddler's son, Philander Perrely."

Two Thousand Dollars!

GIB could hardly believe his eyes. Philander Perrely was the last one he ever expected to see at the meeting, for he always kept away from affairs in the village. What had he come for?

"What do ye want in here?" shouted someone. "Get off'n that window!" There were outcries against Philander. Then a voice sounded out clear, "First time a Perrely's ever brung hisself to hear a preachin'!" And there was laughter.

Philander jumped down from the window onto the back of a pew. There was a scrambling to get out of his way, and some cried out as if afraid. But before anyone could stop him, Philander had run like a tight-rope walker along the pew's back and landed in the aisle. Then he cried out, "There's somethin' I've come to say here."

"Not here," came the constable's voice. "This is an orderly meetin'." And joined by two helpers, he rushed at Philander.

"Leave me be, Mr. Chubb," cried Philander. "Lemme say my piece afore I leave."

"Yes, let him be, Asa," shouted someone, and for a moment the constable paused. "We all know the Perrelys an' Martindales are cats an' dogs."

Gib's father shouted from the platform in a rage, "This has nothing to do with what we're considering. Take him out."

There were cries of objection, especially from those who wanted to see the old family feud come out in the open. "Let Philander have his say, if he kin unstick his mouth long enough," shouted one man above the rest.

There was laughter, for this was a reference to Philander's usual unwillingness to talk at all.

Asa Chubb looked over to Hannibal, who glanced at Gib's father.

"The peddler's son has nothing to say," insisted Sylvester Martindale. "This is not a baiting."

Gib could sit still no longer. He jumped to his feet and fairly shouted over the heads of the audience. "Let him speak. Please let Philander speak."

This came as a surprise to everyone. The struggling

in the aisle stopped, and the clamor was hushed.

"But Gibeon," his father began anxiously.

"No, Father," said Gib. "Philander is my friend."

Sylvester Martindale stared at his son unbelieving, "Your friend!"

"Yes, he is," said Gib, and he turned to Hannibal. "Mr. Sage, please let him speak if he wants to. I want him to, please, sir."

Hannibal turned to the meeting then. "I reckon it's up to you folks. Is he to speak?"

"Them folks in the valley don't listen any of us," said one voice in opposition. Another was more vehement, "We don't want opinions from every low-livin', God-neglectin' . . ." But there were many more who were curious to know what Philander could possibly say on the matter. Constable Chubb and his helpers turned Philander around and marched him down the aisle like a prisoner.

Philander cried out, "Here, let go o' me!" And he shook them off with such violence that one of his captors lost his balance and fell, while Asa Chubb collapsed into one of the front pews on Taverner Gaylord's lap.

The taverner laughed, but Asa struggled to his feet muttering, "What d'ye think ye're doin'?"

Philander shouted, "Maybe ye'd like me to speak my piece from the stocks!" He clapped his wrists together and held them up. "Here, bind up my wrists with rope. Mebbe ye think I kin talk better with chains on."

This was amazing eloquence from Philander, and

many were impressed.

"Let him be, Asa," warned Hannibal. "Come up here, Philander Perrely, boy, and speak your piece."

Philander climbed up beside the shoemaker. Gib caught a glance from Philander, but there was no smile on his face. He looked down at his audience and then up at those in the gallery. He seemed in no hurry to speak. He was almost daring them to interrupt. But everyone was still now. He had impressed them by his sudden burst of speech, and curiosity was uppermost.

"Well," he said finally, "I reckon winter must be a long way ahead for you folks to be sittin' here wastin' the mornin'. Why don't ye listen to the boy and then go home? What's there to argue about? There ain't none of you knows no different. When he tries to tell ye the truth, ye call him a liar. Go on then, call me a liar too. 'Cos I'm goin' to tell ye what he did at the fire. I wuz there."

This piece of information rocked the hall from end to end with a clamor of voices so loud that Hannibal had to shriek with his strange call to get quiet again.

"Go on, Philander! Go on!" shouted half the hall. Philander nodded solemnly and cleared his throat.

"Reckon I see'd the barn smoke risin' 'bout the time Gib Martindale did, for I clumbed a tree up Larkin Rise to get a better see. Could spy the barn from there an' the smoke comin' out o' the door. An' I see'd Gib Martindale runnin' in from the field. See'd him tie his face up with his shirt and go into the barn. I got down an' started a' runnin' down the hill. Time I got there, Gib had most untied the oxen. Come tumblin' out at me as I come up." Philander pointed an accusing finger at his listeners. "Gib saved those oxen. But not Mr. Petit nor none o' you's got no praise for Gib Martindale. Oh no! 'Cos to your skinflint, shriveled-up, miser-eaten hearts savin' dollars like a miser's a whole heap bigger'n savin' lives, ain't it now?"

"Hey, Gib, ye never told us 'bout the oxen!" shouted Jesse Gaylord, and a confusion of voices followed.

"An' he did more, if ye'll stop yellin'," cried Philander.

"Go on, Philander. Go on."

"Well, Gib picked up Mr. Petit's ax an' chopped that fence to save it from settin' fire to the house."

"An' what was you doin', Philander?"

"He was gettin' tired, so I took the ax an' finished the job for him. That's all."

Orasmus Petit was on his feet at once. "If that there's the downright truth, then why didn't the boy say nothin' 'bout Philander's bein' there?"

Philander had already stepped down from the platform and was striding up the aisle. He turned and looked at the farmer scornfully. Everyone waited expectantly.

" 'Cos I asked him not to. That's why. An' he's got more honor than most of you knows anything about."

At that he turned, pushed past the crowd at the doorway, and was gone.

The meeting was for the moment hushed. Sylvester Martindale turned to Gib and demanded loud enough for all to hear, "Is that the truth, Gibeon?"

Gib nodded his head. There were tears in his eyes. Philander had been a real friend. "Yes, sir, it is."

There were murmurs of satisfaction throughout the hall. Hannibal spread out his hands and laughed. "Well, I reckon that takes care o' that. An' Orasmus, I reckon ye kin thank Gib Martindale for savin' your oxen, an' maybe your house as well."

The shouts of agreement won the day. The opposition felt too much set back to raise any objection to forgetting about the vote. The meeting began to break up, with a growing stampede for the door. There was work to be done at home, now that the show was over. But at this point Orasmus Petit let out a high-pitched howl, which sounded to Gib like a fox in a trap.

The excited little farmer danced up and down on the platform, waving his arms about like windmills. Everyone jumped at the sound and turned to see what had happened.

"Wait," screamed Orasmus, "that ain't the end o' the story, by no count." He fairly hurled his words out as he crouched over the pulpit. "If Philander Perrely kin stand up here and tell the whole story so smooth and easy, then I say there's somethin' that hasn't been answered. But the lot of you's like a flock of sheep an' can't do nothin' but lose yer heads and forget to think."

There were shouts of protest.

"If'n that ain't the plain truth," cried Orasmus, "then how is it no one's asked this peddler's son what he was doin' snoopin' around my barn?"

"But he said he saw the smoke from Larkin Hill."

Orasmus laughed in mockery. "Where there's smoke there's fire, ain't there. Why didn't he want no one to know he was there? If Martindale's boy ain't guilty, then I say the peddler's boy is"

But it was easy to see from the reaction that most of the folks in the hall had lost sympathy with Orasmus' accusations. The movement towards the door continued, which set Farmer Petit's fury to a boiling point. He raised his voice a notch higher as he shrieked, "Well, I want an answer. If'n I'm wrong 'bout that, an' if'n this here town can't do nothin', I'm a' goin' straight to the county sheriff. For what was in that box in the barn was my entire savin's. Ain't it a big enough crime fer to rob a man of near on two thousands dollars?"

There was a gasp of astonishment. That was more money than most people in the community had ever set eyes on, at one time at least.

Sylvester Martindale said very little to Gib as they drove home in the chaise. He seemed to be doing a lot of thinking. Gib was glad of it, for he felt tired and was glad to be getting away from the clamor of men's voices. He wondered what his father would do. Would he still insist on punishing him for trespassing on the Perrely property and climbing out of the window?

When they came to the house, Sylvester told Gib to go to the house while he went straight to the barn.

"You go into the house, Gibeon. Your mother'll want to hear all about the meeting."

Mrs. Martindale had, in fact, been watching anxiously out of the window for their return and opened the door at once. She had not gone to the meetinghouse. Not being allowed to go in, she preferred not to hang about outside "with all those gossips," she said.

She took Gib in her arms at his good news and drew him into the house. Lovina had food ready for him, and both women hovered over him as he stuffed himself with corned beef and cabbage, boiled potatoes and turnip, green apple pie and cheese. Meanwhile, in some miraculous way, he managed to tell of the happenings of the meeting.

His mother then insisted on his going up and resting on his bed. "You need the rest, Gib," she said, stroking his forehead, "and I must speak with your father when he comes in."

"Do you think, Mother," Gib asked, "that Father should be talked to now about letting Djulih work here?"

"I just don't know, Gib," she said. "I'll see."

Gib *was* tired. No sooner had he put his head down on his pillow than he fell into a deep sleep.

The next thing he knew he was dreaming about a box of gold coins, that he supposed was Orasmus Petit's savings, lying under a clump of birch trees. The branches shone and shook like scrawny arms, and the wind blew down a cloud of yellow leaves like fire. Gib could see Orasmus Petit sitting on the porch of his old house howling like his own hound. Someone was pulling at Gib's arm and telling him to come away. Then he woke up to find his father standing over him, shaking his arm, "Wake up, Gibeon," he was saying. "We'll go and see Pardon Perrely."

For Gib the ride that followed was the strangest ride he had ever had, even though he was going down a familiar road; for he was going to the forbidden place in the company of his father. It was more like the dream that he had been dreaming, except that this was for him much more exciting. Perhaps it was the first time since the beginning of the feud that Martindales had ever visited Perrelys.

As the chaise turned off the lower road and went in through the crumbling iron gates, Gib looked about eagerly, hoping to see Djulih. But as usual, there was no sign of life. Everywhere there was litter and a mass of choking weeds.

Sylvester Martindale drew the chaise up in front of the house. There was no use knocking on the front door, though. It quite obviously hadn't been used for years. Gib followed his father around to the yard in back, where bits of rusted iron and rotting wood indicated some long abandoned farm implement.

"Needs a bit of house cleaning, doesn't it, Gibeon?" said his father with a chuckle. Gib liked the way he said

it, for he appeared to be mildly amused rather than critical.

They went up to the kitchen door and knocked. There was no sign of life inside. Perhaps the Perrelys were away. His father knocked again, louder. Then he backed up. "Are you sure they live here, Gibeon?" he joked.

At this point the door opened, and Mrs. Perrely stood like a forbidding shadow at the entrance. She looked at Gib's father, then at Gib, then back again at his father. But she said nothing.

"Mrs. Perrely, I'm Sylvester Martindale."

The woman nodded without a trace of greeting. "I know," she said.

"Is Mr. Perrely in?"

There was a pause. The woman seemed to hesitate. At that moment, Djulih slipped around her mother and out of the door. Her face lighted up with joy on seeing Gib. "Gib!" she exclaimed, then she glanced nervously up at her mother and lowered her eyes.

"Show them where Pardon is, out in barn," said the woman and closed the door.

Djulih's face became joyous again as she looked at Gib.

"This is my father, Djulih."

She looked up at Sylvester Martindale. "How d'ye do, sir," she said, and made a quick curtsey.

"Well thank you, Miss Perrely," said Gib's father.

"My pa's over t'barn, workin' on his cart, sir."

Gib could see that his father was impressed by her polite manner. She wore no shoes, and her hair hung down her back, but she had a bright blue dress on that looked new. She led them across the yard to the back of the barn where stood the peddler's cart. There was a bucket of red paint beside it, and the cart was half painted. It was the brightest red color that Gib had ever seen; and he laughed, remembering how Mr. Perrely had said that was what he would do.

But there was no sign of the peddler.

"My father should be here," Djulih said in a puzzled voice. The answer came from quite close, "Reckon he is, too."

It was Pardon Perrely, coming cautiously out from under the cart with a large palm-leaf hat on his head. He had a red paint-laden brush in his hand. His shirt was smeared, and so was the pair of old-fashioned breeches he was wearing. He was bare-legged and bare-footed and ready for a good scrubbing. But he seemed totally unconcerned about his appearance and talked in his sing-song voice as he unstooped himself, stretched deliciously, and came forward.

"An' a fine mess o' color he is, too. But if a critter has to paint himself up like an Injun on the warpath, better it be a fancy color at that, ain't that so, Doctor Martindale?"

Gib looked at his father nervously, but he saw that Doctor Martindale had no intention of putting on a disapproving tone. In fact he laughed and said, "A good coat of paint won't hurt any of us, I'd say."

The peddler looked at Gib and winked, "I heer'd ye sunk into a peck o' trouble when ye got home."

"Philander saved me, Mr. Perrely," said Gib proudly, "by all the things he said."

Pardon Perrely threw back his head and laughed. "The first time I heered that close-mouthed son o' mine doin' anythin' with his tongue."

"But he spoke well," said Gib's father. "Like an orator. I'd like to thank him. I came to thank you all."

"Never counted on hearin' any sech thing from a Martindale."

"I suppose not," said Doctor Martindale, and Gib could see that his father was finding the whole affair awkward, but the peddler went on quite happily.

"Why," he said, "I know'd of a man who lived over to Fiskdale; made his money composing right bang-up an' knock-down curses for folks to use against their neighbors when they'd quarreled with 'em. He made a lot o' money makin' up curses, but he never made no friends. Mebbe now it's time for the Martindales and the Perrelys to stop makin' up curses an' get down to makin' friends."

Sylvester Martindale laughed at that and agreed they should try.

Both Gib and Djulih listened to the way the conversation was going in astonishment. It made Gib long to talk to Djulih alone, so he could tell her everything that had happened. And she must have felt the same. For when Pardon Perrely told Djulih to hunt up Philander, she took hold of Gib's arm and pulled him away with her. Gib looked back at his father, but the two men were discussing the virtues of carriage wheels. This came out of the fact that Philander had thought up a new tire for the peddler's cart, which bound the wheel over the joints of the felloes in one piece.

They make a strange pair, thought Gib, seeing his father dressed so formally in dark frock coat and pantaloons and the paint-smeared, bare-footed, talkative peddler in palm-leaf hat and smeared breeches.

"Will your father have me up at your house?" Djulih was asking excitedly. They were moving in and out of the broken-down Perrely buildings, which seemed to have no purpose in standing at all.

"I don't know," said Gib.

"Didn't you ask him?"

"I told Mother," said Gib. "But up to now, my father wouldn't listen to anything I said; and even now, I'm afraid he's going to say no."

"But he's bein' awful nice," observed Djulih.

"Yes, I know," said Gib trying to pluck up courage to continue the conversation. "Of course, there's Lovina, too. She's got to like you, for you'd be working under her."

"Don't she like me, Gib?"

'She's always muttering about the low-living Perrelys."

"Oh," said Djulih.

"I'm sorry, Djulih, but I have to tell you the truth, don't I?"

Djulih nodded solemnly. "Maybe I kin change her when she gets to know me."

"I'm sure you can," agreed Gib. "She's not really bad at all. Not as bad as Granny Hope."

"Your grandma is she?"

"Yes, but there's nobody on this whole wide earth she likes, I reckon, Djulih; so of course a Perrely is pretty far down in the scale. She spits tobacco juice into the fire every time a Perrely is mentioned."

Djulih laughed at that. "Perhaps I kin change her, too."

Gib made a long face. "She's never got changed by nobody yet."

They could not find Philander.

"He's not in his work shed," said Djulih, "or ye'd hear a lot o' hammerin' or bangin' of things around."

"What does he do in his work shed?" asked Gib.

"Want to see it?"

She did not wait for a reply, but led Gib to the door of the shed and pushed it open. It was very dark in there without a light, but what Gib could see made him think of the blacksmith's shop.

"What is he making?" Gib asked.

Djulih shrugged her shoulders. " 'Bout everythin' ye could think on, I reckon. New inventions mostly."

"What does he do with them?"

"Nothin'," said Djulih casually. "He ain't never had

the money to patent his things, so he's jest kept everything a secret. 'Course now . . ." She broke off suddenly, and Gib picked up the conversation.

"Somebody should finance him," he suggested.

Djulih just laughed. "Who? Philander's nothin' but a low-livin' Perrely. Ain't nobody up in the village kin forget it."

They returned to the two men, who were still talking earnestly.

"I suspicion Philander's off trappin' woodchucks," said the peddler. "No use waitin' fur him. He don't stay around the house much any time."

Gib's father was looking at Djulih. He said, "Miss Perrely, I need extra help at my house. Mrs. Martindale would be really glad to have you come and live with us for a spell. Our Lovina could show you what's to be done."

"Jimminy, Father, that's wonderful!" cried Gib.

"Well," said Doctor Martindale soberly, "Miss Perrely has to decided for herself." He turned back to Djulih. "I talked to your father about it, Miss Perrely."

"Yes, Djulih," nodded the peddler. "Right fine of Doctor Martindale, ain't it now? All arrangements made."

Djulih was overcome with pleasure and a sudden shyness at the same time. She curtseyed to Gib's father with her eyes lowered. "Oh, thank you so much, sir," she said.

It was arranged for Djulih to come to the house a

week from the following Monday. Gib felt very excited, because it seemed as if he had arranged it all himself. He made it his business to prepare for the event by talking to Lovina. But she was wholly non-committal and quite skeptical toward the idea that it would mean less work for her.

"I ain't partial to meddlin' of many hands," was all she would say.

As for Granny Hope, she puffed on her pipe in the chimney corner as if she were building her own private fire. She spat so rhythmically, it seemed to Gib she did it by the clock, every two minutes. But she said nothing. This was her way of being in a fury. There wasn't any point in Gib's talking to her.

A Matter for the Magistrate

MEANWHILE all talk in the village centered on the one question: Who stole Orasmus Petit's savings? It seemed as if the whole community had slowed down. Farming, for this period, became a fitful work. Whole families from outlying areas pulled into the village to clutter up the green with their carts and their patient, pondering oxen. For long periods of the day, they sat around or stood around, in groups of men, in groups of women, while the children ran about screaming. If the community kept this up, there would be starvation ahead for the winter. At least that's what Gib heard the older and wiser men say.

But the whole affair was too rare an opportunity for excitement to let it pass. It meant that the tavern, where the villagers liked to go for lively discussions over rum or cider, was doing a roaring business. Men congregated outside the blacksmith shop and argued and speculated fiercely, with the excuse that they were getting their carts repaired or their oxen shod. Moriah Tibbals had never had so much work in his life, and shoeing oxen was no easy task. All four hoofs had to be strapped down or there would be a lot of unpleasant kicking. All this took time, and resulted in a lot of talking on the mystery of Mr. Petit's barn.

Aaron Coon, too, was kept delightfully busy supplying provisions and tobacco to those farmers who decided to make the general store their center of gossip.

Indeed the whole village seemed to be a place of waiting, with a feeling in the air that something was bound to happen. The village had been deprived of something that only one man had known existed, but this, once revealed, had become the concern of everyone.

In all this excitement, no one noticed the fact that the Reverend Mr. Elijah Bownum had absented himself from the scene. Gib had seen him, dressed in black, trotting off on a black horse on the road toward Worcester on Friday morning. Gib had waved at him, but the parson had kept his eyes glued to the road in front and never relaxed his stern gaze.

The morning after Mr. Bownum had left, Orasmus

Petit came screaming into the village. He sat in his ox cart, addressing anyone he could get to listen. In a few days time, he said, justice would be done. The county sheriff had agreed to come to Sturbridge. The culprit who stole the savings would be caught and condemned.

He might as well have said "executed," Gib thought, for nothing less would satisfy the raging farmer.

The only individual in the community who went about his business unconcerned was the peddler, Pardon Perrely.

He seemed totally untouched by the tension in the village. Proud of his brilliant red cart, hardly giving it enough time to dry, he drove into the village Saturday afternoon. He sang a gay tune under his breath, occasionally resorting to whistling to express a burst of good feeling. He headed straight for the general store.

The buzzing of the many gossipers, sitting, lounging and leaning about the front porch, sank abruptly into silence, alert and curious. All eyes were fixed on the peddler.

Gib just happened to be there, too. He had been sent by his mother to buy two skeins of silk and a bottle of lamp oil. Rags, which his mother and Lovina had collected for months, had paid for the silk, and he had paid for the oil in dollars. He had just come out of the store as the peddler came up. Gib watched, and so did Silas Bushaw, who had come out of the store, curious about the sudden silence.

"Mornin' to ye, gentlemen all," sang out Pardon Perrely as he hitched his horse to the post. "A handsome occasion 'tis for the likes o' me, when I come to buy rather than sell." Then he glanced over the cold faces of his audience and said with a twinkle in his eyes, "But unlike most o' you folks, I don't calculate to haggle at the price."

"It's easy to buy at a price when ye've got the money in your pocket, peddler," drawled Silas.

There was some meaningful laughter, which Pardon Perrely accepted with a lively nod. He seemed unaware that to display one's money at this time was to put one under suspicion.

"Go out on the road, Silas," he said. "You kin find a heap o' money on the road."

"Don't have to go far for it, neither, eh, peddler?" Silas was again rewarded by guffaws of pleasure.

"That's right-down true," agreed the peddler innocently.

He greeted Gib as he passed into the store. "Mornin', young feller. That daughter o' mine asked me to tell ye if I seed ye that she's sure lookin' forward to comin' to the house."

Gib thanked him for the message, but the peddler hardly listened. He marched straight into the store and started buying provisions at such a rate that the crowd outside began to seep into the store to watch. Gib stayed, too, and was dismayed to hear the murmured comments of the onlookers. They all hinted that the Perrely had strangely come into wealth, and linked it up with Petit's stolen money.

Gib could see that the peddler was enjoying himself. He sat on one of the barrels shouting out his needs, sometimes jumping off like a youngster to point closely to something he wanted in particular. His wants seemed to include anything and everything: from coffee and tobacco to threads and yarns, from suspenders and mittens to candles and copper bells for his cart; even sticks of striped barley candy and red and white peppermint drops!

He didn't seem to notice the impression he was making. Either that or he didn't care. Aaron Coon listened soberly to the orders from his customer, showing no expression at all, a contrast to Silas Bushaw who passed so many pointed remarks at the expense of the peddler that the audience began to have a very good time.

At last Aaron Coon turned to his assistant and said sharply, "Bung it up, Silas. Mr. Perrely has a right to buy what he wants for the winter."

"Yes, Mr. Coon," said Silas quickly.

"And help Mr. Perrely get the things in the cart," added the storekeeper. "If you folk will be good enough to stand aside."

He waved the men out of the doorway. Someone started to help get all the goods into the cart. And others followed his example, so that the Perrely cart was loaded in a few minutes. Though everyone made a show of being very neighborly, Gib noticed that they were really smirking behind the peddler's back.

Gib walked home, feeling very uneasy. He knew that all this was leading to trouble. And it came later that day.

First the parson returned, as solemnly as he had gone. He went straight to the tavern to talk to Mr. Gaylord. Rumor spread like wind through the village. An important visitor was to stay at the tavern.

There was a hasty meeting of the selectmen, and Gib's father returned looking disturbed. He called Gib into the parlor and closed the door.

"I'm sorry, Gibeon," he said seriously, "but we are not yet clear of this trouble. The county officials are now fishing in Sturbridge waters."

"Yes, sir," said Gib.

His father sighed. "It means more questioning. Mr. Petit is bringing disgrace on this community, shouting out to the world that we can't manage our own affairs. If the old miser had all that money, you'd think he'd have hidden it in a better place than a barn."

"Who could have taken so much money?" wondered Gib aloud.

"Orasmus Petit is convinced he knows."

"Who, sir?"

"Philander Perrely."

"That's not the truth," cried Gib. "Philander would never do a thing like that."

"Probably not," said his father. "But the Perrelys haven't made it any easier for themselves."

Gib supposed his father was speaking of the peddler's appearance at the general store. And Gib could only agree.

The Sabbath came, bringing an uneasy peace and a solemn lecture about love and forgiveness from the Reverend Mr. Bownum. The peace was followed by renewed excitement. On Monday morning a closed coach and pair, with a coachman on the box, drew up at the tavern door. Riding behind the coach on horseback were two big silent men. It was a sight that set the children all agog. They called out to their parents, who came running. Before the coach door could be opened to let the passengers out, the crowds gathered to see what the sheriff looked like. For everyone was convinced that this was the sheriff called by Mr. Petit from Worcester.

The selectmen and the parson came out of the tavern, following Mr. Gaylord. Gib was not supposed to be there until noon, but he had escaped Lovina's surveillance and kept himself concealed among the throng of people who swarmed to peer at the strangers. It was Mr. Gaylord who opened the coach door, but before he could speak the parson nudged him aside. He spoke in loud greeting to someone inside. "Good morning to you, Thomas. It's good for all of us that you decided to come along with Sheriff Cox."

"Move aside then, Elijah, and let me out," came a voice from the coach, and out stepped a rather short fussy man, who had darting, piercing eyes, under heavy forbidding eyebrows. He was dressed in black in the old manner, with cocked hat, breeches, white stockings, and square buckles on his shoes.

He was helped down by Mr. Gaylord. Then he turned and glared at the wondering crowd. He seemed to disapprove of them. The three selectmen moved up to him, Hannibal Sage in the lead.

Mr. Bownum turned to the selectmen with a gesture of introduction. "This is Mr. Thomas Everts, Justice of the Peace." While the onlookers gaped, awed at the presence of a magistrate, the parson presented the three selectmen and Taverner Gaylord.

Hannibal Sage bowed rather stiffly and said, "Welcome to Sturbridge, Mr. Everts."

The magistrate pierced him with his eyes. "Well let it be short. I don't want ceremony."

Hannibal paused in perplexity. Mr. Gaylord was able to fill in the breach with his explanation that the best room in the tavern had been reserved for him.

"Does it look out on the green, sir?" snapped the magistrate.

"Oh yes, Mr. Everts. In fact, it is that room you see above you with the large windows."

"I must be able to see out," was the short reply, and it left the impression that the whole village would be watched during the course of his stay in Sturbridge.

Two other men climbed out of the coach, the sheriff and a clerk. The sheriff was tall enough to be impressive. But his face was sallow and expressionless, and he hardly talked at all. Indeed his coldness seemed colorless beside the ferreting alertness of Mr. Everts. The clerk was a youngish man, but thin and stooped. He looked bored, even sleepy.

Mr. Everts turned to look at the people around him. His eyes seemed to pick each one out, examine, and drop them in a matter of seconds. He raised his voice a little as he addressed the selectmen. He told them that he intended to talk to many of the townsmen, beginning with the unfortunate Mr. Petit, and without delay. The way he said it, Gib thought, it sounded like a threat.

The magistrate said no more, but marched into the tavern followed by the sheriff, the clerk, and the two aides, leaving Mr. Bownum to explain to the crowd that he had known Mr. Everts since his school days. He had gone to Worcester to invite the magistrate to Sturbridge. The magistrate had agreed to accompany the sheriff, to investigate the case as a favor to Mr. Bownum, but had refused the invitation to stay at the parson's house. "As you will see," said the parson, "Thomas Everts is hardly a man to take things easy. It is an honor for us to have him."

Gib felt rather depressed as he walked home to finish his wood-chopping. This magistrate seemed to be irritated by everything that was done and said. Would he really take time to find out the truth?

Sharp at twelve o'clock, Constable Chubb and one of the sheriff's aides arrived at the Martindale's door to escort Gib to the tavern, even though the tavern was but a stone's throw away.

"Oh dear," sighed Mrs. Martindale, "it does make it look as though Gib was being led away to prison."

"Shouldn't be jumping out of bedroom windows," said Granny Hope, who had not forgiven Gib for his escapade. But Gib paid no attention and went off with as much dignity as he could muster, between two enormous silent men. He held his head high so that no one would think him ashamed, and looked straight in front of him.

People watched the procession go by, but no one dared speak in the face of such forbidding escorts.

As Gib was led into the tavern lounge, where the magistrate sat at a table before the officials of the village, he heard Mr. Everts speak in his rather flat nasal voice. "I'm here to maintain law. That is fixed."

He threw a glance at Gib, then turned to his aide. "Where is this Philander Perrely?"

"Nelson went to get him, sir," explained the aide anxiously. It was clear that Mr. Everts was not a man to be kept waiting.

"It is past noon," he pronounced. "Take the constable with you. Find him."

Constable Chubb and the aide went off to the stable for horses. Mr. Everts hardly stopped speaking, addressing no one, staring at the papers before him.

"Nothing must be allowed to go on that's disorderly. Too much getting out of hand these days. Well, men

may think they change, but the law does not. And if there be any adjustment needed, it will be men that will have to make it, not the law."

As he talked, he constantly sorted and resorted the impressive-looking documents lying on the table before him. Meanwhile, the clerk, sitting at a small table beside him, scribbled with incredible speed, all apparent sleepiness gone.

Without stopping for breath, the magistrate said, "Yes, young feller, you are Gibeon Martindale, age twelve, son of Doctor Sylvester Martindale. Is that right?"

"For a moment Gib didn't realize he was being addressed. Mr. Everts looked up sharply, annoyed at the hesitation.

"Well, well, well? Are you or aren't you Gibeon Martindale, age twelve, son of Doctor Sylvester Martindale?"

"Oh yes, sir, I am," said Gib hastily.

"That's right. That's right. Speak up promptly. If you have been upholding the law, then I can set you free with very little questioning, and you can get back to your games, isn't that right?"

"Yes, sir," said Gib.

The magistrate eyed him sharply. "Why aren't you working? A boy of your age should not be playing games."

"Oh, I'm not, sir. I mean I am working."

Gib looked askance at his father, whose face held a

quick smile of amusement.

"Then," said the magistrate, "you should not have agreed with me when I said you were playing games."

"Yes, sir. I'm sorry, sir."

"I'm not here to play games either. And if everyone thinks they must agree with me, we shan't get anywhere."

Mr. Everts leaned back in his chair. "Now you tell me, Gibeon Martindale, exactly what you did on that afternoon Mr. Petit's barn caught fire. And I will have no interruptions." He glanced meaningfully at Orasmus Petit, who was sitting crouched like a cornered cat in a huge stuffed chair.

Gib told his story well. It was easy now. He had nothing to hide for any reason. The clerk took down his words, he presumed, and Mr. Everts did not interrupt him.

When Gib came to the end, the magistrate said, "And Philander Perrely, this son of the peddler, told you not to speak of his being there."

"Yes, sir."

"Don't you think that odd?"

"He just didn't want to be praised for what he had done, suggested Gib.

"Chopping down the fence? That is not much, is it?"

"But it did save Mr. Petit's house."

"He should be here. Where is he?"

Gib began to say that Philander was hard to find any time of the day, when he realized Mr. Everts was not talking to him, but to his papers.

"Hidin'," said Orasmus Petit. But when the magistrate threw a sharp glance at him, the farmer clamped his mouth shut. Mr. Everts seemed to have him completely intimidated.

There was a pause. The grandfather clock ticked slowly and ominously. Then someone dared speak from the window looking on to the green. "Here comes Asa Chubb."

"The constable that is," explained Aaron Coon, as all heard the rapid pound of hoofs on the road, and the angry cries of geese scrambling out of the way.

Mr. Everts looked at the clock. So did everyone else.

As Asa Chubb moved into the room, red-faced and out of breath, the silence still held. The magistrate stared at him furiously.

"Mr. Everts, reckon Philander's cut off."

"What do you mean?" asked the magistrate coldly.

"Your men are out in the woods, combing for him."

"Wasn't anyone at the house?"

"His mother's there, 'cos the sheriff talked to her. She says her boy says, 'if'n youve got anything to ask him, let ye come down and ask. But he ain't got time . . .' "

"Time!" shouted Mr. Everts.

"Ain't got time to go traipsin' back an' forth to suit every Tom, Dick an' Harry carryin' a load o' curiosity."

Mr. Everts jumped to his feet, pushing the table back with a screech. He stood there without a word, in the silence. Something was going rapidly through his mind, Gib could see that. Then he looked around at the assembly of the village elect, and said quietly, "It is not the law that must change, but men who act under the law. This peddler's son, he has told his story to you all. He came to the meeting house of his free will and fancy to help Doctor Martindale's boy. You see, sirs, there is some good in him. Our object is to find out how large a good that is."

Gib listened carefully, but he could not make up his mind whether these words of the magistrate were good for Philander or not. The next words startled him.

"What I need now is a close friend of this peddler's son. Is there any one of you gentlemen here closely acquainted with Philander Perrely?"

There was a moment's silence. Farmer Petit muttered, "There ain't a soul would be a friend of that low-livin' . . ."

Mr. Everts cut him off. "We all know you are not a friend of the peddler's son, Mr. Petit."

There was some tittering at that, but no one came forward to present himself as a friend of Philander.

Aaron Coon said, "I reckon, Mr. Everts, the family down there don't speak much to anybody."

Hannibal laughed. "You might even say, none of us up here speaks much to them down there."

"Hm," said Mr. Everts. "Trouble always comes out of hard feelings. Men always make the most of hard feelings."

Gib stepped forward. "Mr. Everts, sir," he said in a voice that he had difficulty steadying, "I am a friend of Philander Perrely."

"You!" The magistrate raised his piercing eyes full at Gib.

"Yes, sir."

Gib's father started to interfere, but Mr. Everts waved him silent with an impatient hand. Then he studied Gib for a moment, before he repeated, "You?"

"I'll do what ever you want, sir, truly," pleaded Gib.

"Then I will use you, said the magistrate.

Gib heard Aaron Coon behind him, "This ain't no job for a twelve-year-old." But Mr. Everts ignored it.

"I will make use of your son, Doctor Martindale."

Gib looked at his father anxiously, but Mr. Everts did not wait for an answer. He addressed everybody in the room. "I wish to make it clear that I want nothing done in the neighborhood concerning this case for a day. You present, the selectmen and leading officials of Sturbridge, will generally inform everyone of this order. Those living in the village will stay in the village, that is, not go beyond the green. Those living on farms beyond will stay on their own land. I will ask all of you present to appear before me at noon the day after tomorrow. Until then, I want no one to be found near or about or on the Perrely lands. If anyone is found disobeying these orders, he will be regarded as embroiling himself in the case we are considering, and therefore at once subject to imprisonment, under suspicion of abetting a crime. My words have been taken down by my clerk. He will repeat them to the selectmen on request. Good-day, sirs."

He made a short bow from his place at the table, then moving round he took Gib's father by the arm and led him to the end of the room. Gib didn't know what the conversation was about, but in a moment his father nodded and moved back to him.

"You are to stay here, Gibeon. Mr. Everts will tell you what he wants you to do. What ever it is, I hope you will conduct yourself with honor, as you have done so far."

"Yes, sir, I will."

Sylvester Martindale patted his son on the shoulder and followed the rest of the men out. Only Orasmus Petit had the boldness to stay in the room. He began to address the magistrate, complaining that nothing was being done to get his money back. Mr. Everts was not kind to him.

"You're in my hands, Mr. Petit, whether you like what I'm doing or not. Have patience, sir, and try to keep your temper. Good-day."

The Important Errand

GIB could never have dreamed he would become so important to the village. He had a mission to do. Only he could do it. He was not allowed to discuss it with anyone, not even his own family. When he left the tavern that afternoon, his stomach aching for want of dinner, he was escorted home by Constable Chubb, who said nothing to him, but treated him with a new respect.

When he got home, he found dinner awaiting him. His mother and Lovina had been told by his father not to ask him questions. So instead his mother kept clasping and unclasping her hands, while gazing at him from

154

across the table as if she thought he had been elected representative to the government in Washington. Lovina heaved herself in and out of the kitchen, repeating to Gib, "Eat. You will need to eat." Granny Hope, from her place in the chimney, kept glancing over to him with suspicious looks, forgetting even to spit.

Early the next morning Gib went to the barn to saddle Marybell, with full permission from his father. He rode off with stacks of food in his saddlebags, his whole family at the door to see him off.

His way led down the road and around the corner past the meeting house; and all along he could see people looking out of their windows and doors at him. It was a gray day. Rain was in the air, but the cool wind made Gib feel alert and happy, just as Marybell was. It was only when he got to thinking about what he had to do that he became serious.

Gib decided not to hold to the road, but to press through the meadows and pastures. He knew the land well and had no difficulty avoiding the thickets, but he found the way he had chosen was unusually soggy. Marybell was soon having her problems. In the end he had to come round the low-lying area in a slight detour. It was land not far from Orasmus Petit's house.

Gib was keeping Marybell at a cautious walk when he was startled by a sudden crash of branches off to one side. This frightened Marybell, too, for she veered so abruptly away that Gib almost lost his seat.

At first he decided he had startled a group of deer.

He turned to investigate, hoping to catch sight of them. But instead he came upon a small clearing by a stand of white birch. Near the roots of the trees, he saw an old hat that had been blown by the wind so that it was caught against the looping arms of a blackberry bush. It was made out of palm leaves. As he held Marybell in check, his ears caught the sound of running feet.

Who could it be? Gib pressed Marybell on and soon came out on a rocky ledge, which gave him a view down the valley. There was not much to see but a mass of tree foliage with faint suggestions of fall coloring and now and again some bare patches of rocky ground. Gib surveyed the scene until suddenly his eyes caught some movement less than a mile below. The next thing he knew he was watching a man running down the slope, for a moment in full view.

From that distance the man looked stocky in build, though he was crouched forward as he ran so that the impression was hardly reliable.

Gib moved on, full of wondering. Mr. Everts had given definite orders that no one should wander around today. And why should the man be running? Gib's thoughts went back to the clearing where he had heard the first sound. He decided he would go back there and investigate as soon as he had a chance. Then he wondered, too, if the hat had belonged to the man who was running away.

He had been foolish not to pick it up. It looked like the old palm leaf hat worn by Pardon Perrely as he painted his wagon. In an uneasy, fleeting moment he thought of the peddler. Surely that could not have been Djulih's father running off down the slope, though the man had been going in the direction of the Perrely land.

Gib spurred on Marybell, intending to hurry on to the road and gallop down to the bridge. Perhaps he could overtake the man.

When he arrived at the bridge, he was stopped by one of the sheriff's aides.

"What's your name?" he asked.

"Gib Martindale."

The guard nodded him on.

"Did you see a man running along this way?" Gib asked.

"When's that, boy?"

"Oh, about half an hour ago."

"No. What man?"

"I don't know. I thought I saw him from up the hill aways."

"Never saw nothin'," said the sheriff's aide, and he looked Gib up and down curiously.

Gib moved across the bridge, puzzled. Of course, if the man didn't want to be seen he would hardly be foolish enough to cross by the bridge when he could as easily wade across the shallows of the river.

Gib took a short cut across the Perrely land and tethered Marybell long before he reached the house. As usual there was only stillness and silence around the house and yard.

What was he to do? If he went to the back door and knocked, he would be greeted by Mrs. Perrely, and she would not tell him anything. He decided to hide and wait. He settled himself in a patch of weeds near a pair of crumbling wheels that had belonged to some long-ago cart.

Gib could see smoke rising slowly from the house chimney. The kitchen fire had not been allowed to go out. Someone was home. He had been sitting in a crouched position for some time, beginning to feel cramped and slightly damp, when the door of the house opened slowly and Mrs. Perrely came into view. She stood for a moment inside the door, tall, erect, and still, as if listening rather than looking. Then her face turned slowly and her dark eyes seemed to rest on the cart wheels. Gib kept every muscle in his body still. There was no expression on her well-shaped face. As always she looked grave, and, he decided, sad.

She turned away and moved across to the barn where Aaron Coon had been. As soon as she was gone, the door of the house opened again; and Gib watched as Djulih came darting out and around the house. She was wearing an old brown dress with an apron over it, and she carried a basket, which she clutched in her arms.

Gib wanted to rush out and follow her, but he feared her mother would come out and see him. He had to wait several minutes before the woman reappeared and crossed over to the house.

As soon as the door was closed behind her, Gib cautiously withdrew from his hiding place and made a circuit around to the front.

There was no sign of Djulih. He went some yards away and called her name softly. There was no answer. He looked for signs of her trail. But there were none. He felt he was wandering aimlessly and wished he had stayed at the house to watch for her return. Not knowing what else to do, he began calling Djulih's name again, much louder.

After the second call, he heard a sound. Turning, he saw Djulih standing, watching him. There was a look of her mother about her that Gib had never noticed before.

"Djulih," he said. But she did not move towards him.

"What d'ye want here?"

Gib was stunned by her evident unfriendliness.

"Why, Djulih," he said, "I . . . I was calling for you."

"Get on home, Gib Martindale. It's better that way. The village don't want us, and we don't want to have nothin' to do with them."

Gib said desperately, "That isn't true."

"Yes, it's true, or they wouldn't have the sheriff and his men huntin' for Philander like he was a animal."

"But Mr. Everts—he's what they call a justice of the peace—he only wants to question Philander."

Djulih's eyes flashed. "Well, ye kin tell your friend Mr. Everts that Philander's not interested in that kind o' questioning."

"Djulih!" exclaimed Gib forlornly. "Why do you talk to me like that? I thought we were friends, you and I."

"Didn't that justice man send you here?"

"Yes, but . . ."

"Then we ain't friends. An' ye kin tell your pa I'm not comin' to your house after all. I don't need to. Didn't need to before. We got money now. I don't need anythin' your kind kin give me."

Gib's heart sank. Did the Perrelys really have money? Had Pardon Perrely really come home from his trip with large sums of money? And if he had, couldn't the Perrely's see that it was a dangerous thing to come into money at this particular time when Orasmus Petit had just lost his?

His horrified thoughts caused Gib to hesitate. Djulih turned and was about to leave. But he couldn't let that happen. "Djulih, Djulih," he called, "please don't go. I must talk to you. It's awfully important."

Djulih paused, and something made her turn to him again. "What the sheriff and all his lot says ain't important to us Perrelys."

"Oh, Djulih!" exclaimed Gib. "You're prouder than the Martindales. Prouder than Granny Hope, and I never could see what she got out of being so proud."

Djulih looked at him sharply, then grimaced into a reluctant smile. "Well, we've got a right to be proud, too, if we want to be."

"But Djulih," Gib pressed on, "please don't be so

proud that you can't talk to me. Maybe I'm doing what's wrong. If I am, surely you can show me."

Djulih stared at him. He could see he had reached her at last, though she said, "If ye be takin' the sheriff's part against us Perrely's, then it's wrong, dead wrong, Gib."

"But I'm not doing any such thing. I have a message to give to Philander. That's all. He only has to listen. If he doesn't want to do anything about it after he's heard, then that's up to him. Where is he, Djulih?"

She looked at him with a terrible coldness, and said, "An' if'n I tell ye where, ye'll tell the sheriff?"

Gib went hot in the face; he felt as if he had been slapped. Without thinking he reached out and seized Djulih by the arms. Taken by surprise, she tried to spring back, but he held her tight even though he knew he must be bruising her arms. "That's a low-down thing to say, Djulih!"

"Let go," was all she said.

"Philander came up of his own choice to the meeting house to help me when I was in trouble. Do you really think I'd betray him?"

"So you would if'n they'd prove him guilty o' somethin'."

"Prove him guilty!" Gib stared unable to say more.

She struggled to be free of him; and when he saw that there were tears in her eyes, he let go, feeling suddenly helpless.

She turned away from him, but, to his surprise did

not move away.

"Djulih," he said softly, still afraid that she might run off, but not knowing how to hold her.

There was a pause, then she turned, wiping her eyes with a quick move of her wrist. "I love my brother, Gib. He don't deserve havin' folks huntin' him as though he was nothin' but a beast."

"I know that, Djulih. I want to help him. Please let me see him."

Djulih hesitated.

"And I'm sorry if I lost my temper and hurt you, Djulih. I can't stand to have somebody tell me I can't be trusted."

She did not reply directly, but said in a low voice, "They think Philander stole Mr. Petit's money."

Gib pointed out to her that it was only certain people who thought that. And not Mr. Everts. "Why he's even against Mr. Petit and shuts him up every time the old miser opens his mouth."

"Then why are the sheriff an' his men huntin' my brother?"

"They're not, Not today. Don't you see, Djulih, Mr. Everts didn't have to send me down here to talk to Philander. He could have left it to the sheriff, got help from the village, called on the county officials, and beaten the woods for Philander. But he doesn't want to do that. He just wants to talk to Philander."

"Philander's not goin' up there. It ain't safe for him."

"Please trust me, Djulih."

Gib could see that she was beginning to give in. She looked at him with large worried eyes, then turned half away and nodded her head. "I will then. He's up in Devil's Den."

"Where's that?"

"I'll take you," she said, almost under her breath, and began to walk across the meadow. Gib followed. She said nothing more to him, but pressed on at a great rate until they were soon climbing a steep slope where jutting ledges of rock looked out on the slopes below. Djulih made a point of peering back every so often to see if they were being followed.

Gib had never been this way before. The Devil's Den turned out to be a small cave cut out of limestone cliff.

Some yards away from the opening, Djulih stood and called Philander's name. It was easy to see why, for Philander came out of the cave with his gun in his hand. He seemed very tall as he unbent and stood with his legs astride. His face was expressionless, and he made no comment as Djulih explained to him that she had brought Gib along with her.

She moved forward and gave him the basket. He looked across at Gib, nodded, and as he sat on the ground, motioned for Gib to sit beside him. There was bread and meat in the basket, which Philander proceeded to tear into with his teeth.

Djulih stood a little apart, watching her brother with evident satisfaction. Gib waited for Philander to speak to him. This was not until most of the meat had been eaten. He wiped his fingers on his pantaloons and speared the bread with his hunting knife.

"Gib Martindale, what's brung ye up here to my devil house? Han't been no other's gone to this much trouble to find me. Begun to feel lonesome, reckon." And he laughed as if it was easy for him to make a joke.

"The magistrate, Mr. Everts, sent me," said Gib.

There was a pause. Philander tore at a chunk of loaf. Then he said, almost casually, "Are ye workin' for him, now?"

"Not against you, Philander." Then Gib explained how he came to be out looking for him with a message from the magistrate. Philander listened closely, and Gib tried his best to describe the man as he really was.

When he had finished, Philander laughed shortly. "I'd sure liked to see Orasmus Petit with a bung in his mouth. But I couldn't come yesterday. I was over to Worcester."

"What ever did you go there for?" asked Gib.

"Ain't none kin steal my inventions now, 'cos I've applied for patents on six of 'em."

Gib was full of wonder. "You mean you've invented six things that nobody's ever thought up before?"

"Reckon," said Philander casually. "They's still others. But six is enough as a start."

Djulih moved closer and sat down to listen.

"I've heard you've made something for your gun to better its aim," said Gib looking across at the weapon lying on the other side of Philander.

"That's one o' them," said Philander, and he took hold of his rifle to show Gib. On the curve of the barrel as it ran into the stock there was an iron projection pierced by a sighting hole. It could be raised or lowered by the turning of a screw. This simple device, in the hands of a marksman like Philander, made his gun the most accurate weapon anyone in the county had seen or heard of.

"Then there be somethin' for a spinnin' frame, like at the mill I worked at oncet," Philander went on. "Often carve 'em out o' turnips an' potatoes first to give me the right shape. Did that for my idea for a mould-board for a plow. Lot better'n them bull plows. Made one finally meltin' iron in a potash kettle lined with clay. Mebbe ye don't know 'bout sech things, Gib, but it's a heap o' fun to do when ye know how."

"How long did it take you to think them up?" Gib asked, for the moment forgetting all about his mission.

"Oh, for some years I've been shapin' up things."

"You could be a rich man, Philander, couldn't you?"

"Well, it ain't no use buildin' things to see others come along an' steal 'em from under your nose. It's patents that keep 'em your own. But I han't never gotten patents afore 'cos I ain't never had the money to pay for 'em."

"Where did you get the money?" Gib said it, and then wished he hadn't. He realized at once it was the wrong thing to ask.

"I hain't stole it from crabby Petit's barn, leastways."

"Of course I know that," Gib said quickly. "I didn't mean that."

"I suspicion they mean that in the village."

Out of her long silence Djulih said, "It's our father's come home with the money."

"Yep," said Philander with a note of pride. "Reckon he come home with more'n he ever made afore. Thought of my inventions right off first. Said I should go without waitin' on the sheriff. First things first, he says. No use waitin' on the law to clap ye into jail for havin' a face that looks like it's stole somethin'."

"But what are you going to do now?" asked Gib.

"Jest sittin', waitin' for the storm to blow over. Don't aim to sit in no county jail to please ol' Petit none."

"But, Philander, you'll be found here if they really start searching. And they will if you don't go an' see Mr. Everts tomorrow."

"Reckon I'd ruther sit in a hole in the ground waitin' for 'em to give up, than sit in a jail house waitin' for 'em to let me out."

"That's what he said you'd say," said Gib, finding it necessary to get to his feet to talk better.

"Did he?" Philander showed no emotion. "That's what makes him smart, I guess."

"And he said it was exactly what your enemies would want you to say, too."

"Why for?"

"Well, he said a man who runs away is always thought to be guilty, whether he is or not."

"I ain't runnin' away, stayin' here."

"If you don't go to see the magistrate when he wants, just like my father had to do, like I had to do, like everyone he said he wanted to see, then that's considered running away. What can Mr. Everts do then but to go out and look for you?"

"What if he don't find me?"

"Philander, don't you see what will happen? He's the judge of the whole county. He and the sheriff can round up hundreds and hundreds of men, just by asking for them. And they'll come pouring over the land with bloodhounds and everything, like Mr. Tibbals says they do in the South when a slave runs away. And you won't have a chance. And by that time the whole world'll say you're guilty of running off with Mr. Petit's money."

Djulih listened to Gib's story with an expression of growing fear, but Philander sat stolidly looking out across the valley in deep silence.

Gib went on desperately. "Don't you see, Philander? Mr. Everts doesn't want to do that. He's called off the search instead, for a whole day; and he's ordered everyone to stay away, stay in their homes."

"Don't make sense," said Philander.

"It's because he wants you to have a chance to come in of your own free will and talk to him before it's too late. That's why he wanted a friend of yours to come—someone you trusted, he said—to try to make you see how terrible it would be for you to stay away. Don't you trust me, Philander? I told him you did. I know I'm kind of young to put your trust in. But please, please do."

Philander was silent for a long time. Then he got up and stretched. "Well, Gib," he said solemnly, "reckon I'll go do it. Leastways for you I will."

Gib felt weak with relief. "Oh good," he said.

Philander spoke quietly. "Now you go on back. An' ye tell this here Mr. Everts I'm comin'. Where's he stayin' at?"

"At Mr. Gaylord's tavern."

"Tell him I'm comin' this afternoon. An' crabby Petit, nor Aaron Coon, nor no one else'd better fool with me when I get there. It's the magistrate I come to see, an' I ain't talkin' to no one else."

Hidden Gold

THE sun had risen almost to its highest point in the sky, with the clouds beginning to thin out, as Gib reached the bottom of the valley. Djulih was still beside him. There was a shininess of damp leaves and fresh grass all around, a time meant for joy, but Gib was too filled with worry to be joyous. He guessed Djulih felt the same way; for, beyond asking once if he really felt it was safe for Philander to go up there, she was silent.

Gib was relieved to find Marybell where he had left her. She was tethered, but somehow he had half expected to find her stolen by the mysterious man he had seen running. He smiled at his own wild imagination

170

as he untied the mare. Then he turned to Djulih.

"Djulih, do you know where your father was this morning?" The question came out of a suspicion he could not get rid of, even though he felt ashamed of it.

"My pa?" she asked surprised, then she nodded quickly. "Oh, I reckon I do. He was off along the river makin' a picture of it."

"Oh," said Gib.

He looked back when he reached the road and saw Djulih standing just as he had left her, in the middle of the grasses. She was staring at him, frightened, and yet wanting to have trust. Gib waved to her, but she did not wave back, or turn away.

Gib went across the bridge, where the sheriff's aide raised his hand in recognition. "Did ye come on him?"

"Yes," said Gib. "He'll be coming past in a little while to see Mr. Everts."

The man stared, surprised. "Eh, yes?"

Gib was glad he had told the man; otherwise he might have taken it into his head to try to arrest Philander.

When Gib rode into the village, he found the green full of folks ready to fire questions at him. He shook his head and took Marybell at a proud gallop past them all.

At the tavern, Jesse was there to take hold of the bridle. "The news must be good. I can see it in your face," he said with a laugh, and he led Marybell away to the stable.

Mr. Everts' clerk was at the door. He led Gib straight to the magistrate's room. The sheriff was sitting before the window, an uneaten meal spread out on a small table beside him. He had a cigar in his mouth and seemed lost in a dream.

Gib had a feeling that everything all over the land was held at a standstill by this man's sitting here. He seemed to have an uncanny control over the movement of life. But would he be able to find the real thief, or would he allow himself to be swayed by the judgments of others?

From the depths of his heavy stuffed chair, he said, "Leave me, Josiah. I'll have this young feller alone."

As soon as the clerk had closed the door, Mr. Everts made a gesture toward the upright chair facing him. He did not look at Gib; his eyes were fixed on the distance.

"Philander Perrely's decided to come," said the magistrate matter-of-factly. "I knew he would." Then he turned to Gib a moment. "Oh, that's not to say you haven't done a good job, boy. I knew you'd do that, too. You had to persuade him a mite, eh?"

"Yes, sir,' said Gib. "He still believes it's just a trick of yours to put him in jail."

"Don't ever be a judge, Gib Martindale. He's the one man that's always condemned long before the trial starts." He motioned towards the dinner. "Lookee, eat. I haven't the stomach for it now."

Gib hesitated. He had forgotten the food put in his saddlebag, and he was getting hungry. But it didn't seem right to eat Mr. Everts' meal.

"Eat, boy," said the magistrate insistently. "I don't want to hurt Mrs. Gaylord's feelings, and she cooked it herself."

Mr. Everts watched Gib eat. His piercing eyes under the heavy brows looked sad. "When is he coming?"

"This afternoon he said, sir."

"Where did he get that horse?"

"Horse?" Gib was puzzled, then he realized Mr. Everts was speaking of something out of the window. Two horses were galloping up. Even at such a time, it was impossible for Gib not to be excited at the sound of fast galloping. He hurried to the window and saw Philander drawing up at the tavern and leaping off a roan horse. Behind him was the sheriff.

Philander had his gun in his hand. He was dressed in black, his best clothes, Gib assumed, brought out for the occasion. In them he looked very tall and handsome, and as usual very solemn.

Mr. Everts got up slowly and stretched. "Best leave me alone with him, Gib Martindale. Philander Perrely and me's got to have a long talk."

Gib turned in sudden fear. "He didn't do it, Mr. Everts. I know he didn't."

"I hope you're right, boy. I hope you're right," was all the magistrate said.

Gib met Philander in the entrance hall of the tavern and raised his hand in greeting. Crowds had formed outside, shouting and jeering, frustrated at being kept from coming in by the two aides and Taverner Gaylord and his son who stood guard at the door.

"Well, I'll meet your friend the magistrate now," said Philander as he passed, but he did not smile.

Gib sneaked out the back way and found himself walking toward the mill pond, a half-formed idea in his head. He was thinking of the birches and the old palm hat caught in the bramble. If he went there without delay, there would be no one about and he could be back before anyone knew it. He hoped he could be back before Mr. Everts had finished with Philander. He walked cautiously at first. But feeling the pace too slow, he broke into a run. Hurrying too much, he constantly ran into thickets and caught his clothes on unseen thorns. The series of small detours he was forced to make confused him, and he began to wonder whether he would ever find the clearing. But at last he went up to his ankles in swamp land. Then he remembered where the place was, and he turned the way he had gone with Marybell, moving around a stand of pines.

Gib approached the clearing with great care, moving only a short distance at a time, always listening for sounds. But there were none. Finally he stepped into the clearing and stared. The hat was gone.

Cautiously he moved forward. There had been no wind strong enough to blow it any distance. Someone must have taken it. There were no tracks that he could see, but his eyes rested curiously on the ground near the roots of the birches.

Suddenly it came to him that those branches covering the spot were not growing naturally. They had been twisted round and woven into each other so that the ground at the tree roots was covered.

He crouched down and examined the ground underneath. There were signs of earth scrapings. When he put his hand down and pressed at the earth, he felt it give. Behind it was a space that extended under the roots of the tree. He pushed his hand in and felt something solid, metal. It was not large, and he found he could draw it out.

He pulled it cautiously into the light of day. It was an iron box, which opened easily to Gib's fumbling. Then he stared for what must have been minutes without moving. Before him were gold coins. Masses of them. Here certainly was the painfully hoarded money of miser Orasmus Petit. The coins sparkled in the light, and when Gib moved his fingers to touch them, he did it as cautiously as if he were putting his fingers to a shining fire.

He could hardly contain his excitement as he closed the box and pushed it back under the trees. He wanted to leave everything just as he had found it. He felt somehow that this would be Mr. Evert's wish. The thing he must do was run back and tell Mr. Everts.

He turned and was about to start back for the village the way he had come when he thought he heard a sound. His first thought was that the thief had come upon him. He prepared to run for his life. But then he caught a glimpse of a brown form disappearing into the stand of pines beyond.

He called out wildly and gave desperate chase, but when he parted the branches he could see no one in the silent cave-like gloom under the trees. He called again. His voice was like a wild sob. "Djulih." Had she seen him with the stolen money? What was she doing there?

There was nothing but silence, and the silence oppressed him. A little beyond him he saw a fallen pine trunk and walked cautiously over to it. He peered over. Djulih was crouching behind the log, her face buried in her hands.

"Djulih," he said, "what are you doing here?"

She looked up at him, her face distorted with fear and anger. But she did not answer.

"Djulih." He leaned down and shook her gently by the shoulder. "How long have you been here?"

But she shook her head as if she had lost her voice.

"Djulih, have you been watching me? Did you see . . . ?" It suddenly struck him that she now believed that he had stolen the money. "Djulih, you don't think that I hid the money there?" He shook her more desperately now. "Djulih, you can't believe that!"

She turned her head away. He got down on his knees and tried to get her to look at him. "Look, Djulih, we have to talk. Please come with me, and we'll move away from here. It's dangerous to stay near that money. The men who stole it might come back, and if they find us here, they might . . ."

He broke off, and she turned to stare at him, as if surprised. He got up and pulled at her arm. She did not resist him now, and he took her by the hand and led her out of the pines and around the marsh.

He found a hummock that the sun had made warm, and they sat down. Listen, Djulih, while I tell you how I found the money."

She nodded, although she kept her face turned away from him. He plunged right in, beginning with the man he had seen running and the palm hat that had disappeared. When he got through, she turned slowly and looked at him. "I'm sorry," she said, so softly he could barely hear her.

"Sorry, Djulih? About what?"

"I thought when I see'd ye there that it was like Mr. Petit done said—ye stole the money. An' I thought, that ye'd got Philander up there to be jailed instead o' yourself. You see," she went on, "I reckon I'm so scared on account o' my brother, I jest can't think proper."

"Oh, that's all right," said Gib with a sigh of relief. "But it's a right good thing that no one else saw me; for not many would believe the truth like you, Djulih, and I'd be in the county jail next thing for years."

"Is that where they'll take Philander?"

"Djulih, Philander's not done anything wrong! Mr. Everts would never put Philander in jail."

"I was goin' up to see for myself," she said, "an' come this way to stay off'n the road."

"Well, you come with me now, Djulih. We must tell Mr. Everts about the money. That should save Philander, if he needs any saving."

"How'll it save Philander?" asked Djulih doubtfully.

"Well, the money's found now."

"But that don't say who stole it outer Mr. Petit's barn."

Gib looked at Djulih for a moment. "Eh, Djulih, that's true!" He was disappointed.

It was agreed they would go to Mr. Everts just the same and tell him at once.

The Fight

WHEN Gib and Djulih got to the village green, they found the tavern surrounded by most of the village folk. There were a good many stares at the sight of the Martindale boy walking with one of the Perrelys. Willis Pickle, who was with a group of his school friends, sidled up to Gib to tell him the latest news, while staring at Djulih to watch her reaction.

"Mr. Everts has arrested Philander Perrely on account of him takin' the old miser Petit's gold."

Gib's face flushed. He heard a gasp of horror from Djulih beside him, and he shouted at Willis in a rage, "That's a low-down lie!"

180

"What's a lie?" screamed Willis. "That he did it, or that the sheriff's got him?"

"Both."

"What ye gettin' so ugly about, Gib?" jeered Willis. "Ye brung Philander up here yourself so's the sheriff could arrest him, didn't ye?"

That pleased Willis' friends a great deal, and they clucked and crowed like a barnyard.

"I didn't bring him here to be arrested, and he didn't do it either," shouted Gib.

"Well now, Gib Martindale, reckon you'd best not defend him too hard from now on."

Gib saw that Djulih had started toward the tavern door. "Get out of my way," he cried at Willis, for the boy had established himself square in the way, with the other boys crowding round.

"Well, now, ye ain't thinkin' of making me, are ye, Gib?"

Gib could see that he was being riled, but the jeering faces of the other boys made him swallow Willis' bait. He threw his weight forward and shoved Willis out of the way. But Willis turned and grabbed his arm. The next minute they were wrestling fiercely and beating wildly at each other with their fists.

A fight was just what the other boys had been waiting for. They roared their enthusiasm and quickly formed a circle. Even while he was struggling with Willis, Gib was cursing himself for being such a fool. This was not the time to get into a fight. And he was not sure he could get the better of a boy so much heavier than he.

One of his flying fists caught Willis in the face, and drew blood. Willis came at him like a raging bull, pressing Gib back into the yelling boys, who punched Gib in the back. Someone tripped him. He stumbled, and felt the weight of Willis coming down on top of him. Gib guessed that Willis was a whole lot stronger, but that he was also so blinded with rage that he fought without good sense, exhausting himself with aimless violence. Gib tried to keep his own brain clear.

They rolled over and over on the stony ground like a couple of wild cats. At a moment when Gib found himself on top, he jumped away. Willis made a lunge at his feet, but Gib came down on Willis' shoulder with such force that the boy went sprawling. His head hit the ground. He was apparently stunned, for he lay there, breathing hard, making no immediate attempt to get up. The other boys stared, unbelieving.

Gib did not wait for more, but charged into the crowd of men hugging the tavern door. His name was being called. It was his father, who reached out and seized him by the arm.

"Gibeon, what's the matter with you?" He hauled Gib into the tavern. "I looked out of the window and saw you fighting like a wild Indian out there. This isn't the time . . ."

"Willis said Philander stole the money," Gib protested sullenly.

"Well," said his father, "Philander's being held."

Gib stared at his father appalled. "But you don't think . . . Mr. Everts doesn't think he's really guilty. He couldn't."

"I'm sure Mr. Everts knows what he's doing, Gibeon."

"But he's not guilty. I know him. He couldn't be."

Doctor Martindale shook his son, raising his voice sharply, "Look here, boy, stop being a little fool. This is not a game. Two thousand dollars worth of money is missing. Somebody's got to be guilty."

"Could I speak with Mr. Everts," Gib said, remembering the hidden money. "I must speak with him."

"No, son, you cannot. Nobody can see him. Not until tomorrow."

Gib felt suddenly depressed. What could he do? Everything seemed to have gone wrong. The fact that he knew where the money was would not help Philander in the least. The only one to gain by his telling about it would be the miser Petit, and in his present mood Gib did not feel Orasmus Petit or anyone else deserved to see that money again. He didn't care if the thief, himself, whoever that was, went and got it. It would serve them all right.

Doctor Martindale, as one of the selectmen, was too busy to spend time with Gib. "Sit here, Gibeon," he said sternly. "I will be finished in a while, and we will go home. Tomorrow, Mr. Everts is having a public hearing at the tavern here. You will have to attend, of course. The way he talks, he may turn it into a trial."

A trial! Gib wondered what that would mean. Did Mr. Everts really mean to sentence Philander to prison? Gib sat down in the chair his father indicated and gazed miserably around the room. There was no sign of Djulih. The selectmen were going over some papers. A notice of the tavern hearing was to be given out. It had been decided to use the ballroom of the tavern. The building itself would be guarded back and front by the sheriff and his men, with the help of constables brought in from the neighboring villages.

Rumors of all this had leaked out long before the selectmen were finished, and the crowds began to thin out as people returned to their homes. They were mostly gone by the time Gib came out of the tavern with his father and went round to the stables to claim Marybell. There was still no trace of Djulih, and Gib wondered what she would do. Would she tell someone about the hidden gold? But who was there to tell such a story to? Gib hoped she wouldn't. He realized now, it would more than likely hurt Philander's postion still further, and Djulih would be considered an accomplice.

Gib, glad his father was silent, pressed his head against Marybell's neck, feeling the warmth of the animal as comfort. He envied her simple life, which had no worries in it, no responsibilities and no sorrows.

As they approached the house, Doctor Martindale turned to Gib. "Gibeon," he said, "no matter what the sheriff decides about Philander, I still want Djulih to come to the house. We have no quarrel with the Perrelys now. Folks have to learn that."

"Thank you, sir," Gib said solemnly, but in his heart he doubted that Djulih would want to come to the house now. No matter how she thought things out, she would always have the feeling that her friend and the friend of her brother, that is he, Gib, a Martindale, had betrayed them.

"Should Philander be proved guilty, Gibeon," his father went on, "it'll be for one reason—a lack of schooling. A man without education nowadays will always have things against him. This we must understand. Djulih's only a girl, but she needs schooling, too. And I'll make it a point to see that she gets it, along with you."

Gib was overwhelmed by the change in his father. "Oh, that's fine," he said. "Djulih's always wanted to go to school. She told me."

Gib didn't want to do any talking that evening. He found his mother's concern about his obvious gloom annoying. She could not help him with her consolings and cuddlings. Lovina stomped around saying nothing, but looking as if she were saying over and over: "You see, I told you, you can't trust a Perrely." As for Granny Hope, she was almost boisterous, chirping to herself in the corner about things that no one could have understood, even if anyone had bothered to try.

Gib finally said he was tired. His father gave him what seemed to be a smile of understanding, and Gib hurried off to bed, almost letting the candle go out in his haste to get upstairs and be alone with his thoughts. But he found there was little he could think constructively about. His one conclusion before he went to sleep was that as a last resort he could always take Mr. Everts to the hidden money and let him think he, Gib, had stolen it. That would save Philander from years in jail anyway.

Courthouse in the Tavern

THE ballroom on the second floor of the tavern had been arranged specially for what was loosely being called a "trial." Taverner Gaylord had been around the neighborhood and had managed to scrape together enough benches and chairs to fill the room.

All the important men of Sturbridge were there. Gib imagined how he would have enjoyed the sensation of being one of them, if it had not been for his feeling of despair.

There were two chairs on either side of a raised platform. On the platform there was a table for the use of Mr. Everts and his clerk Josiah. On the table was

188

the gavel brought over from the meetinghouse to re-
mind those present that this was to be a sober, orderly
meeting. Beside the table was an upright chair. Gib
assumed this was where Philander would sit while he
was being questioned.

There was a feeling of great solemnity about the
gathering, quite different from the disorganized,
emotional affar at the meetinghouse. Everyone wanted
to get in, of course, but there was little pushing and
shoving. As the men entered the tavern, they were
ushered into the ballroom one at a time by the taverner,
himself, and his son. Tibbals the blacksmith and his two
sons, the Reverend Mr. Bownum, the lean-faced Aaron
Coon, Hannibal Sage the shoemaker, Jonathan Pickle
—Willis' father—one leading townsman after another
came in as Gib watched. Orasmus Petit stomped into
the room holding a walking stick like a sword. When
Pardon Perrely came in, Gib was dismayed to notice
that the peddler had become worn and stooped, his
habitual good spirits for the first time torn from him.
He found a seat in the back of the room and looked
at no one.

When all were seated, the sheriff and one of his men
came in and took the seats on either side of the platform. They were followed by Josiah the clerk, who
slid into the room with his writing sheets and arranged
himself for endless scribbling at the table. Finally, Mr.
Everts appeared at the door, garbed in black as usual.
His black eyes darted fiercely about the room. The

sheriff and his aide sprang to their feet. The door of the room was closed by Chester Gaylord, who came in behind Mr. Everts and quietly took a seat himself.

Satisfied that everything was well under control, Thomas Everts crossed to the table with quick short steps. Quiet filled the room as he spoke in a whisper to the sheriff, who promptly went out of the door.

There was no sign of Philander. Gib imagined him chained in some locked room, sitting in hurt silence as he waited to be taken away to the county jail.

"Citizens of Sturbridge . . ." That was a strange beginning, Gib thought. "Citizens" was meant only for people who lived in a city. Was Mr. Everts trying to make the men of the village feel important? It seemed so, for he went on to stress the gravity of the situation: a village that had, for many years, even generations, kept for itself a spotless reputation, had suddenly found itself the victim of a foul crime. The money was not really the important thing to anyone but Mr. Orasmus Petit, and yet Mr. Petit was one of them, part and parcel of the community. "What is done to him is done to all of you. Not the loss of money, but the sudden tearing down of trust, of security, of neighborliness and respect for the law. Without the law no one, no man, woman nor child, can be safe."

When Mr. Everts came to the law, it sounded to Gib like a reference to the shattering of the Ten Commandments, as if thunder and lightning should roll in condemnation of what had been done. Even the parson could not have said it better from his pulpit.

"Now, Elijah," he said, turning to the parson, "all of us are present to decide in sincerity the nature of the truth. May we have a prayer that our hearts may be found honest in judgment."

The parson prayed earnestly, but his words seemed pale before the eloquence of Mr. Everts.

After the prayer, Mr. Everts rose from his chair and made a sign to his aide. The man immediately went to the door and opened it. Philander was pushed rather roughly into the room by the sheriff and Constable Chubb. Philander looked at no one. He kept rubbing his wrists, and Gib from his seat near the door was dismayed to see the marks of a rope on his skin. So they had even tied Philander as though he were a dangerous criminal!

Philander was escorted to a seat a little aside from the front row, so that he sat alone, facing Mr. Everts.

The sheriff went to the door and locked it. He turned then, facing the room, his legs astride, his arms folded. Constable Chubb and the sheriff's aide stood on either side of the magistrate's table.

"Now," said Thomas Everts flatly, "you can see by this that the door is locked and the law is not to be evaded. You folks before me, every man jack of you, is in effect a prisoner of the law."

There was some uneasy stirring, but no one dared say a word.

"I do not intend to go over ground covered already,"

the magistrate went on. "But there seem to be a number of questions unanswered, whether deliberately or unconsciously. I intend to have them answered. When my clerk here calls your name, please come to the front and sit in that chair." He indicated the empty chair beside the table. "I will have you cooperate with me by answering my questions to the point. There is no time for speeches or any expression of opinion unasked for. Is that agreed to?"

The question took everyone by surprise, and there were murmurs of uneasy assent.

The first one to be called to sit in the chair was Philander Perrely. Gib watched Philander with amazement, for he hardly seemed the same person. Sitting in the chair he was thoroughly subdued, meekly answering every question put to him. It almost seemed as if his spirit had been broken as a result of his capture by Mr. Everts and the sheriff.

"You've been needing money for a long time, haven't you, Philander?" Mr. Everts asked.

"Yes, sir," Philander said, his eyes on the floor.

"What for?"

Philander looked up at his questioner in surprise.

"Tell them," said the magistrate.

"I've been wantin' to take out patents on my inventions. Couldn't market 'em without patents or someone else'd be stealin' 'em."

"Patents on what?"

"A gun sight and a churn and a self-workin' mule

for a spinnin' frame, a mould-board for a plow, somethin' for a pump, an' somethin' for a morticin' machine."

"How do you know so much about machines, Philander?"

"Worked in a shop some years back at Lowell."

"What made you leave the job?"

"Was forced to leave, 'cos I was caught takin' one o' them frames apart."

"Why were you doing that?"

"I was aimin' to find out how they could be bettered, I guess."

Thomas Everts got up from his chair and moved in front of the platform to face Philander. "When I arrived in Sturbridge, I sent out an order for you to come and see me. Did you get that order?"

"Yep, reckon I did."

"Did you come to me?"

"No, I went to Worcester."

"Why?"

"To patent those things o' mine."

"You had the money? It costs money."

"Yes, sir."

"It was what you've been wanting to do for two years, isn't it?"

"That's rightdown true."

"But you never had the money before. Now you had it."

"Yes, sir."

"How did you get it?"

This was the key question. Everybody watched intently. It did seem that Philander hesitated a moment before he answered. "My father gave it to me."

"He had the money, and he gave it to you?"

"Reckon so."

"Yes or no, boy."

"Yes."

"All right, Philander, you go back to your place now, and let me question your father."

"Mr. Pardon Perrely," announced the thin voice of the clerk.

The peddler seemed like a man in a dream, quite unsure of himself. His nervousness was evident long before he spoke, for he kept pulling at his fingers and crossing and uncrossing his legs. He spoke so low it was often hard to hear him, and the magistrate had to ask him to speak more plainly.

Yes, he did have quite a lot of money when he returned from his traveling, and he gave his son enough for him to get the patents. It was what his boy wanted, and he had a right to it. Mr. Everts interrupted constantly as the peddler began rambling on.

"But where did you get that money, Mr. Perrely?"

"Brung it back with me. Jest got back from travelin' up an' down the coast sellin'."

"But you'd never been able to do this for your son before."

"No, never before, I didn't."

"Why not?"

"I ain't jest capable to say."

"But you made more on the road this year than any other year."

"Yep, I made considerable . . . a deal o' money . . ." His voice faded out.

"How do you explain that, Mr. Perrely?"

"Did more business, I calculate. Business whole lot better all over. Such things comes an' they goes. Nothin' that nobody knows on. Dunno myself 'bout sech things. I only knows when I sells, I sells."

He rambled on again until he just faded out without Mr. Everts doing a thing to stop him. When the silence came, it was broken only by a single sigh from the peddler.

Mr. Everts spoke up then. There was a sharpness to his voice. "Why don't you tell me the truth, Mr. Perrely?"

The peddler looked up startled. His lips worked as if forming words, but nothing came out.

Mr. Everts moved closer to him. "You didn't get that money selling copper kettles, wooden clocks, straw brooms, or anything else you had on your cart for bartering, did you?"

The peddler stared at the magistrate's face a moment as if unable to speak. There wasn't a man in the room who didn't hold his breath for fear of missing what Pardon Perrely would say. Mr. Everts wasn't a man to be fooled by anyone.

"Well, Mr. Perrely, tell us: How did you get that

money?" The magistrate folded his arms sternly.

The peddler dropped his eyes and twisted his hands in a frenzy of agitation. Judging by the stirrings in the audience, some had decided that the trial was already over. They were stunned into new silence by the peddler's mumbled words.

"It was them paintin's, Mr. Everts. I'm sorry, sir."

"Paintings?"

"Folks seem to like what I do for 'em in colored paints."

"What do you do, Mr. Perrely?"

"I copy their faces for 'em, or their whole selves, and make a picture of it with a pretty wooden frame around it."

"And people pay you to do that?"

"Yes, sir. Seems like they like it an' pay me a good deal. More'n I think they should, for it don't take me long an' I like doin' it so it comes easy-like. Reckon I like doin' it more'n anythin' else in the world, I guess."

His voice had trailed off again. But the silence in the room, Gib realized, meant that everyone was listening. This was a new side to the peddler. Nobody had known he was an artist. Why he could become famous— famous as Gilbert Stuart for instance, who had painted the first President.

Mr. Everts spoke abruptly, turning away. "You may go to your place now, Mr. Perrely."

Pardon Perrely got up slowly to go, then turned.

"Why do ye prison Philander, Mr. Everts?"

"No, no question from any of you," was the quick reply.

"But . . ." began the peddler with slow persistence.

"Ask me that tonight then."

Pardon Perrely stared. "After ye've taken him away?" But as Mr. Everts did not answer, the peddler shrugged his shoulders and crept back to his seat.

"Mr. Orasmus Petit," said the clerk.

The farmer was ready, as usual, for an opportunity to accuse. He had been shut up so many times by Mr. Everts that it must have seemed like Divine Providence to have the magistrate question him for a change.

The first question was a surprise to everyone. "Well now, Mr. Petit, tell me why you were not in your house when the barn caught fire."

"Eh," shrieked Orasmus, almost jumping out of the chair, "it didn't catch fire; it was set afire."

"Mr. Petit," snapped the magistrate, "confine yourself to my question. Why were you not in your house?"

"I was out pickin' my cabbages."

"The garden is far from the barn, then?"

"Not so far."

"Could you see the barn from the garden?"

"I could see."

"Then why didn't you?"

"See the low-down thief? 'Cos when Philander Perrely there went into the barn . . ."

Mr. Everts interrupted him sharply, "I don't want any opinions, Mr. Petit."

"Opinions? Ye asked me, didn't ye?"

"I didn't ask you who went into the barn."

"Who? Who else but Philander . . ."

"Do you want me to discount your words altogether?"

"What's that?" queried Petit, frowning.

"If you, Mr. Petit, insist on being judge and executioner, as well as witness and accuser, I shall have you forcibly ejected from this room."

"Well, I don't know . . ."

"You are right, sir. You don't know. A man is condemned by facts, not opinions. Just answer my questions."

The farmer was silent, his eyes darting about the room.

Mr. Everts motioned to the sheriff, who strode up to Petit's chair. The farmer sprang to his feet in sudden fear.

"Hey, ye leave me be! Are ye jailin' me now?"

Mr. Everts persisted. "I will have an answer, Mr. Petit. I say it for the last time. Are you prepared to answer my questions plain and simple, stating the facts as you know them, *without* opinions?"

"Yes, Mr. Everts. I . . ."

"Good," snapped the magistrate. "Now sit down."

Orasmus Petit sat down subdued. The sheriff went back to his post at the door.

"Now, sir," pressed the magistrate, "you didn't see any person enter the barn while you were in the vegetable garden. Is that right?"

"I didn't see no one."

"And you did not see anyone enter the barn after you'd finished in the garden?"

"No, Mr. Everts, I couldn't neither, since I left with Aaron an' the wagon."

"Mr. Aaron Coon that is?"

"That's right. Went with him to his general store here in the village."

"Why?"

"Well, ye see, he was to pay me fur the goods, an' . . ."

"Mr. Coon didn't have the money with him?"

"No, Mr. Everts, he didn't."

"And you left the farm with him in his cart to go to his store and receive the money?"

"That's the way it was, Mr. Everts."

"That's when the barn was burned."

"That's rightdown true, for when I got back 'twas most charcoal."

"Do you leave your farm often, Mr. Petit?"

"Next to never, I calculate. This was first time I kin remember in most a year."

"Thank you, Mr. Petit. Go to your place."

"Mr. Aaron Coon," said the clerk.

Aaron Coon walked solemnly to the chair.

"Mr. Coon," began the magistrate quietly, "is it true that on the day of the fire you were buying vegetables from Mr. Petit?"

"Yes, Mr. Everts, that's true."

"Had you bought vegetables from Mr. Petit before?"

"Every year. His vegetables are very fine. I kin sell 'em in my store easy."

"And you pay him in dollars, rather than barter, because Mr. Petit is known to be fond of money, isn't that so?"

Aaron Coon smiled, as did most of the men present. "That's right enough, Mr. Everts. I reckon Orasmus will agree with the rest of us there."

"Then why did you fail to bring the money with you when you went to Mr. Petit's farm, since you knew he would accept nothing else in payment?"

Aaron Coon paused a moment and frowned. "Well, I reckon I jest forgot, Mr. Everts. I had tallow in my cart to offer him in exchange."

"You offered him tallow for candles, and he refused?"

"No, I remembered he'd want to have the money."

"Are you in the habit of forgetting?"

"No, can't say I am." Aaron Coon was obviously displeased.

"Your store, Mr. Coon, does it remain open when you go out gathering provisions?"

"Usually, yes."

"Who looks after it?"

"Silas does. Silas Bushaw there."

"Your assistant?"

"Guess you might call him that."

"Was he tending to the store when you returned with Mr. Petit?"

"No."

"Why not?"

"He was sick."

"You mean he stayed home because he was sick?"

"That's right, Mr. Everts."

"What was the matter with him?"

"Just sick. Can't justly say what of. Ye kin ask him, I reckon."

"How did you know he was sick?"

"Well, he didn't come to the store that day."

"You decided he was sick, and that was all right?"

"Well, guess it ain't all right if a young feller's sick. But I ain't no doctor, Mr. Everts."

"Is Mr. Bushaw often sick?"

"No, I can't say that he is. He's a good worker."

"Then for him to be away, it must have been something really bad."

"Mebbe so."

"But he never told you what it was."

"If he did, I don't remember. Maybe he did, but I don't remember."

"Thank you, Mr. Coon. I'd like to talk to Mr. Silas Bushaw."

Philander Uses His Gun

THE clerk repeated solemnly, "Mr. Silas Bushaw."

When Silas Bushaw got up and took the chair in place of Mr. Coon, he seemed different from any of the earlier witnesses; for Silas was a bit of a swaggerer. His eyes looked over his audience as if he despised them all, and he submitted to questioning with an attitude of boredom. Yes, he had been sick on that day, as Mr. Coon had said. What was the matter with him? Well, he wasn't rightly sure. He didn't care to call in Doctor Martindale and pay him just for the name of a sickness. He had known he would get better. He always did by just resting up. It was only something wrong with his stomach, anyhow. He had eaten the wrong thing, he guessed. Did he know about the fire when it happened? Oh yes, of course. He had dressed and come down and gone out to see it. But that was afternoon and he had been much better. "Mrs. Tibbals can tell you that."

"Good," said Mr. Everts at once. "I will ask her."

Silas looked sharply at the sheriff and, for the first time, hesistated.

But his cocksure air came back immediately; and he swaggered back to his place, his thumbs stuck in his waistcoat pockets.

An aide unlocked the door and called out for Mrs. Tibbals to appear. She came in almost at once. It was obvious to the men present that this appearance had been carefully prepared, and that Mr. Everts was working according to a plan.

Mrs. Tibbals, like her husband the blacksmith, was a Quaker who attended the Friends Meeting House on Sabbaths. She was quiet and kind. Most folks liked her. She was the only woman allowed to be present at the gathering, and she knew it well. She tripped in very demurely, but with no hesitation. She kept her eyes lowered, only looking up when Mr. Everts greeted her very politely and led her by the hand to the chair.

"Mrs. Tibbals," he said, "I want you to answer one or two questions. All of us present will be very much interested in your answers."

"Yes, Mr. Everts, I will answer thee." She smiled sweetly and devoted her entire attention to him.

"Mr. Silas Bushaw occupies a room in your house, isn't that so?"

"Yes, Mr. Everts. He has done so for more than a year now."

"Is he a good boarder, Mrs. Tibbals?"

"Oh yes, I can assure thee of that, though I cannot approve of his ways. But then I have told him so many times."

"Well, we cannot go into that here, Mrs. Tibbals."

"No, no, and perhaps it is just that he's full of spirit, as so many young men are these days."

"Yes, well, now, Mrs. Tibbals, I want you to speak of the day Mr. Petit's barn burned down. Did Mr. Bushaw go out that day?"

"Oh, yes, he did. He went to see the fire. So did I."

"That was in the afternoon."

"Yes."

"At what time?"

"At about five o'clock, I calculate, Mr. Everts."

"Did Mr. Bushaw leave the house before that time?"

"Well, he did not leave for the general store that day as he was complainin' some of an upset."

"He stayed in bed until five o'clock when he got up to see the fire, is that it?"

"He was in the bed in the morning. I know because I went up with some breakfast, and he would not eat."

"Did he explain what was the matter, Mrs. Tibbals?"

"Yes. He said he was sick and that he would not go to work and would stay in bed for the whole day. And he would not eat anything. He said he knew he should not eat, because he could cure himself by fasting."

"Did he say he didn't want you to bring him anything to eat all day?"

"Yes, he did."

"And you were not to go up to him again?"

"Yes, he did say that."

"And did you do as he said, Mrs. Tibbals?"

"No, I did not."

"Why was that?"

"I was worried about Mr. Bushaw, and I thought perhaps he would change his mind about eatin'."

"When did you go up the second time?"

"I calculate around noon time."

"Was he there?"

"He did not seem to be. The door was locked, and he did not answer when I called."

"Not there?"

"I was there. I was asleep." The sudden interruption came from Silas at the back of the hall.

"How do you know?" asked the magistrate turning to Silas.

"I slept most of the day, of course."

"Mrs. Tibbals, is there any way he could climb out of the window?"

Silas Bushaw laughed.

But Mrs. Tibbals nodded her head calmly. "The room is on the second floor, but there is a tree growing very close to the window. A young feller like him could climb easily into the branches and let himself down by the tree."

Mr. Everts turned to the blacksmith. "Is that so, Mr. Tibbals?"

"It is so, sir, whether Silas did it or not."

"And could he climb back the same way?"

The blacksmith laughed. "Well, I reckon he's done it more'n once already."

"Of course I have," scoffed Silas from the back. "But why should I on that day, me sick like I was."

"Not so awfully sick it seems," said the magistrate, "since five hours later you were running to the fire."

Silas was on his feet. "See here, Mr. Everts, just what're ye doin'? Tryin' to make me guilty?"

"I haven't the power to do that, no. If you aren't guilty, then you won't get riled up."

Silas sat down again with an expression of disgust on his face.

"Mrs. Tibbals," said the magistrate, "one more question."

She smiled at him again. "Yes, Mr. Everts."

"What was Mr. Bushaw wearing when he went to the fire?"

"Why," she said brightly, "I remember that well. He was wearing his old clothes. He don't wear them often, he being a bit of a dandy, as young fellers are."

"And did he wear a hat?"

"Oh yes," said Mrs. Tibbals at once. "He wore one of them palm hats."

"Palm hats, Mrs. Tibbals?"

"Yes. Sold at the general store by Mr. Coon. Made by Philander's mother, poor thing, when she needs the money bad. I know because I have spoken to her . . ."

Mr. Everts raised a hand to stop her and made a sign to the constable. Constable Chubb stepped to the cupboard and produced a palm hat, which he handed to the magistrate.

Gib stared in amazement. It was exactly like the one he had seen caught in the brambles.

"Is this it?" asked Mr. Everts.

Mrs. Tibbals smiled, nodding her head. "Why, I do declare, Mr. Everts! It do look the very one!"

Aaron Coon spoke up loudly, "You should know, Mr. Everts, that I sold quite a number of those hats. Even the peddler wears one."

"Even the peddler!" repeated the sheriff slowly, as he examined the hat. "Well, I don't calculate this would exactly fit Mr. Perrely, do you?"

There were some smiles from his audience, for the peddler had a lion-like head with a great bush of hair. The crown of the hat in Mr. Everts' hand was quite small.

"Maybe you men here would like to try it on," the magistrate went on, darting penetrating glances into the faces of his listeners. His eyes rested on Silas a moment. "Perhaps, Mr. Bushaw, you would do us the honor of trying it on first."

"I don't see what that would prove," said Silas.

"Well, it might prove that it would fit."

"What about Philander?" cried Silas, who was getting more and more agitated.

"Philander Perrely?" said Mr. Everts. "Well, that's a thought. Mr. Philander Perrely, will you step up here and try the hat on?"

Philander rose from his chair deliberately and took the hat from the magistrate; but he never raised it to his head, for at that moment there came a shout from several present. The window at the back of the room had been flung open, and Silas, with the ease of a cat, leaped over the sill onto the roof, then jumped to the ground one story below, and was gone.

"Stop him!" shouted the sheriff. There was a rush for the window, with cries of, "Stop him, stop him!"

The aides unlocked the door and ran out. The room was a confusion of voices and movement. Everyone was scrambling to get out and down the stairs, as if the tavern was on fire. Doctor Martindale went with them. Gib tried to follow, but was thrown to one side in the press and fell to the floor in the path of Aaron Coon, who seemed frantic in his desire to get past. Gib heard the storekeeper shouting something at him, and he managed to scramble out of the way of stampeding feet.

The younger men of the gathering had followed the example of Silas and climbed out of the window. When Gib got to his feet, there were but four men left in the room.

At the back, slouched in his seat as before, was Pardon Perrely. It almost seemed as if he had no understanding of what had happened. In the front of the room was Philander, acting as though he were still a bound prisoner. At the table were Thomas Everts and his clerk. The magistrate had an expression of grim satisfaction on his face. He seemed unconcerned at the sudden emptying of the tavern, and was meticulously putting his papers in order.

He handed them to the clerk and looked at Philander. "Thank you, Philander. Now you'd better go and explain to your father that you agreed to let yourself be arrested to help my case."

"Yes, sir," said Philander, and he turned to go to his father.

Gib ran forward with a cry of joy, "Philander, you're free then!"

Philander turned to him. "Reckon so, if Mr. Everts says it." He smiled.

Gib turned impetuously to the magistrate, who was looking at him now. "Oh, Mr. Everts, I'm sorry sir."

"Sorry?"

"I did really doubt you, sir. I . . . I . . . You see, I did think you'd really arrested Philander."

"Well, I did. It's always a good idea to do things that set the guilty ones off their guard."

"Then did Silas Bushaw really steal the money, Mr. Everts?"

The magistrate let out a sigh. "Looks that way."

"But you've let him escape."

"Can't do anything about that, Gib. No way to arrest him. Can't prove he did it well enough for any court to send him to jail."

Gib became suddenly excited. "But Mr. Everts, he'll go straight to the money under the tree and go off with it."

"What?" Mr. Everts jumped to his feet. "Under what tree?"

"But I thought," Gib began, "because you'd found the hat . . ."

"The hat? Yes, the sheriff found Bushaw skulking in the woods yesterday, strictly against my orders, and gave chase. The sheriff didn't catch Bushaw, but he did get his hat."

"But didn't he find the money, sir?"

"The money? Petit's money?"

"I know where it is, sir."

Gib had never seen Mr. Everts so stirred up. He seized Gib by the arms and shouted at him, "Where? Where?"

"Under a clump of birch, at a clearing beyond the pines."

"Can you show me, Gib?"

"Yes, sir. I think so, sir."

Mr. Everts rushed to the cupboard and pulled out a gun, Philander's rifle. "Philander," he shouted. "Come with us. If I'm going to find someone to finance this sighting invention of yours, perhaps you'd better prove that it works."

The peddler came running forward, like an excited child. "Yes, yes, Mr. Everts, my son will do it. My son will do it."

"Mr. Perrely," snapped the magistrate, "you can help me, too. Go to the front door and talk to the folks that are out there. Keep them occupied. We'll try to get out the back way without being noticed."

The ruse worked, for Pardon Perrely was delighted with his role and attracted so much attention at the front door that everyone came running to see what was happening. Gib led Mr. Everts and Philander into the woods.

"Lead us as fast as you can, Gib, without breaking into a run, and as quietly as possible. How far is it?"

"About a quarter of a mile beyond the swamp, sir," said Gib.

"Well, wherever that swamp is," said Mr. Everts, "don't go beyond it."

Gib felt like an Indian scout leading the law to the place of the enemy. What if he should lose his way? But he knew that such a disgrace was not to be when his feet began to sink into marshy ground. He stopped and whispered into the magistrate's ear, "It's across there, Mr. Everts. Beyond the pines there's a bit of higher ground where the birches are."

"Good boy," said Mr. Everts. "We'll move into the pines. Keep low and lead the way. And take it slow. I don't want any sound."

Once they got into the pines, it was easy to move silently. Only the fallen twigs had to be watched. Mr. Everts took the lead as they approached the clearing, and motioned to the others to get down on their knees. They crawled to the edge of trees, Mr. Everts ruining his black breches and white stockings, Philander nervous of his best suit, and Gib far too excited to worry about the condition of his clothes.

They peered out. Gib pointed to the white birches, a little distance away. There was no sign of life. But this might be deceptive. It was not possible to see the base of the birch trees because of a scattering of boulders. They would have to move higher up the slope. They began a cautious move from boulder to boulder.

As they reached the last boulder and peered round, they were startled by a sudden cry and a wildly shrieking voice.

Both Mr. Everts and Philander stood up. Gib knew before he looked that it was the voice of Djulih. He saw her now, struggling wildly with Silas Bushaw. She was screaming at him, "Don't touch that money. 'Tain't yours. You stole it. You stole it."

Silas flung her off so that she fell backwards to the ground. He pulled out his hunting knife. "Stay away from me," he shouted hysterically. "Stay away or I'll kill you."

But Djulih seemed to have lost all sense of caution; she moved towards him as he raised his knife.

Gib called out in horor, "Djulih!" But at that mo-

ment there was a sharp report of a gun. Silas dropped his knife, clutching wildly at his wrist.

Mr. Everts ran forward, while Philander stood, legs astride, calmly cleaning the barrel of his rifle before stuffing more gunpowder in with the ramrod.

"Silas Bushaw," warned Mr. Everts, "you're under arrest. I advise you to come quietly. The law is not kind to prisoners who try to escape arrest. Besides, Philander Perrely there's got a gun that never misses."

There was no need of these words, for Silas, nursing his bleeding hand, had lost all urge to fight.

Djulih rushed over to her brother, crying, "Philander, you're freed!" And she threw her arms about him, so that he almost dropped his gun.

"Mind the powder, girl!" he shouted, but realized there was nothing he could do and wrapped one arm around her, grinning.

She turned to Gib. "Eh, Gib, ye brung 'em both! I didn't know what to do. I didn't know where to go. I thought I would guard the money . . . Then I saw Mr. Bushaw takin' it!"

At a sign from Mr. Everts, Gib picked up the iron box. He opened it and showed Mr. Everts the gold coins inside.

"There is Mr. Petit's money, sir."

"I didn't want any of it," said Silas suddenly. "It was Mr. Coon's idea from the first. Like as he thought of burnin' the barn and layin' the blame on them low-livin' folks of the Hollow. He knew where the money was hid and more than oncet allowed as how all that gold could burn up a barn jest by settin' there too long."

"One thing leads to another," sighed Mr. Everts. "But we'll get Doctor Martindale to attend to your hand first. Lead us back, Gib."

Gib led the way, with Djulih beside him. Silas followed in glum silence with Mr. Everts and Philander behind him.

"I aim to come up to your house on Monday, Gib," said Djulih. "Do ye think your pa'll still have me?"

Gib smiled with delight. "Of course," he said. "He's told me so already, and he wants to send you to school with me, too, if you want."

"Oh yes," cried Djulih. "An' I'll learn to read an' write like you."

"Yes, Djulih, and I won't let anyone poke fun at you because you're just starting."

"Thank you, Gib," she said, and actually skipped beside him for a moment, like a little girl just at the age to start school.